(1814-1880) W.H.G. Kingston

Happy Jack

ANd Other Tales of the Sea

(1814-1880) W.H.G. Kingston

Happy Jack
ANd Other Tales of the Sea

ISBN/EAN: 9783744714655

Printed in Europe, USA, Canada, Australia, Japan

Cover: Foto ©Andreas Hilbeck / pixelio.de

More available books at **www.hansebooks.com**

AND OTHER

Tales of the Sea.

BY

W. H. G. KINGSTON,

AUTHOR OF "RONALD MORTON," "THE CRUISE OF THE 'FROLIC,'"
"THE AFRICAN TRADER," ETC.

———➤○◄———

London:

GALL AND INGLIS, 25 PATERNOSTER SQUARE,

AND EDINBURGH.

PRINTED
AND BOUND BY
GALL AND INGLIS
LUTTON PLACE
EDINBURGH

CONTENTS.

PAGE

HAPPY JACK :—

CHAPTER

I. I GO TO SEA IN RATHER UNROMANTIC
SURROUNDINGS, ... 7

II. A STORM, ... 18

III. ON THE RUSSIAN FRIGATE, ... 27

IV. ON BOARD THE AMERICAN BRIG, ... 35

V. OLD TOM'S STORY, ... 42

VI. THE BRIG BLOWN UP, ... 64

VII. A STRANGE DISCOVERY, ... 73

VIII. I REACH HOME, AND THINK I HAVE HAD
ENOUGH OF THE SEA, ... 79

THE "SAN FIORENZO" AND HER CAPTAIN, ... 87

ORLO AND ERA, ... 104

"' It's Jack come back,' answered my sisters and Grace in chorus."— *p. 80*

HAPPY JACK

A TALE OF THE SEA.

CHAPTER I.

THE "NAIAD."

HAVE any of you made a passage on board a steamer between London and Leith? If you have, you will have seen no small number of brigs and brigantines, with sails of all tints, from doubtful white to decided black—some deeply laden, making their way to the southward, others with their sides high out of the water, heeling over to the slightest breeze, steering north.

On board one of those delectable craft, a brig called the *Naiad,* I found myself when about fourteen summers had passed over my head. She must have been named after a negress naiad, for black was the prevailing colour on board, from the dark, dingy forecastle to the captain's state cabin, which was but a degree less dirty than the portion of the vessel in which I was destined to live. The bulwarks, companion-hatch, and other parts had, to be sure, once upon a time been painted green, but the dust from the coal, which formed her usual cargo, had reduced every portion to one sombre hue, which even the salt seas not unfrequently breaking over her deck had failed to wash clean.

Captain Grimes, her commander, notwithstanding this, was proud of the old craft; and he especially delighted to tell how she had once carried a pennant when conveying troops to Corunna, or some other port in Spain.

I pitied the poor fellows confined to the narrow limits of her dark hold, redolent of bilge water and other foul odours. We, however, had not to complain on that score, for the fresh water which came in through her old sides by many a leak, and had to be pumped out every watch, kept her hold sweet.

How I came to be on board the *Naiad* I'll tell you—

I had made up my mind to go to sea—why, it's hard to say, except that I thought I should like to knock about the world and see strange countries. I was happy enough at home, though I did not always make others happy. Nothing came amiss to me; I was always either laughing or singing, and do not recollect having an hour's illness in my life. Now and then, by the elders of the family, and by Aunt Martha especially, I was voted a nuisance; and it was with no small satisfaction, at the end of the holidays, that they packed me off again to school. I was fond of my brothers and sisters, and they were fond of me, though I showed my affection for them in a somewhat rough fashion. I thought my sisters somewhat demure, and I was always teasing them and playing them tricks. Somehow or other I got the name among them and my brothers of "Happy Jack," and certainly I was the merriest of the family. If I happened, which was not unfrequently the case, to get into a scrape, I generally managed to scramble out of it with flying colours; and if I did not, I laughed at the punishment to which I was doomed. I was a broad-shouldered, strongly-built boy, and could beat my elder brothers at running, leaping, or any other athletic exercise, while, without boasting, I was not behind any of them in the school-room. My father was somewhat proud of me, and had set his mind on my becoming a member of one of the learned professions, and rising to the top of the tree. Why should I not? I had a great-uncle a judge, and another relative a bishop, and there had been admirals and generals by the score among our ancestors. My father was a leading solicitor in a large town, and having somewhat ambitious aspirations for his children, his intention was to send all his sons to the university, in the hopes that they would make a good figure in life. He was therefore the more vexed when I declared that my firm determination was to go to sea. "Very well, Jack," he said, "if such is your resolve, go you shall; but as I have no interest in the navy, you must take your chance in the merchant service." "It's all the same to me, sir," I replied ; "I shall be just as happy in the one as in the other service ;" and so I considered the matter settled.

When the day of parting came, I was as merry and full of fun as ever, though I own there was a strange sensation about the heart which bothered me; however, I was not going to show what I felt—not I.

I slyly pinched my sisters when we were exchanging parting kisses, till they were compelled to shriek out and box my ears—an operation to which I was well accustomed—and I made my brothers roar with the sturdy grip I gave their fingers when we shook hands ; and so, instead of tears, there were shouts of laughter and screeches and screams, creating a regular hullabuloo which put all sentimental grief to flight. "No, no, Jack, I will have none of your tricks," cried Aunt Martha, when I approached with a demure look to bid her farewell, so I took her hand and pressed it to my lips with all the mock courtesy of a Sir Charles Grandison. My mother! I had no heart to do otherwise than to throw my arms round her neck and receive the fond embrace she bestowed upon me, and if a tear did come into my eye, it was then. But there was another person to whom I had to say good-bye, and that was dear little Grace Goldie, my father's ward, a fair, blue-eyed girl, three or four years younger than myself. I did not play her any trick, but kissed her smooth young brow, and promised that I would bring her back no end of pearls and ivory, and treasures of all sorts, from across the seas. She smiled sweetly through her tears. "Thank you, Jack, thank you! I shall so long to see you back," she whispered ; and I had to bolt, or I believe that I should have begun to pipe my eye in a way I had no fancy for. My father's voice summoned me. "Now, Jack," he said, "as you have chosen your bed, you must lie on it. But remember—after a year's trial—if you change your mind, let me know." "No fear of that, sir," I answered.

"We shall see, Jack," he replied. He wrung my hand, and gave me his blessing. "I have directed Mr. Junk to provide your outfit, and you will find it all right." Who Mr. Junk was I had no conception ; but as my father said it was all right, I troubled my head no more about the matter.

My father's old clerk, Simon Munch, was waiting for me at the door, and hurried me off to catch the Newcastle coach. On our arrival there he took me to the office of Junk, Tarbox, & Company, ship-brokers.

"Here is the young gentleman, Mr. Junk," he said, addressing a one-eyed, burly, broad-shouldered personage, with a rubicund countenance, in a semi-nautical costume. "You know what to do with him, and so I leave him in your hands. Good-bye, Jack, I hope you may like it."

"No fear of that, Mr. Munch," I answered ; "and tell them at home that you left me as jolly and happy as ever."

"So, Master Brooke, you want to go to sea?" said Mr. Junk, squirting a stream of tobacco-juice across his office, and eyeing me with his sole blood-shot blinker ; "and you expect to like it?"

"Of course I do ; I expect to be happy wherever I am," I answered in a confident tone.

"We shall see," he replied. "I have sent your chest aboard of the *Naiad*. Captain Grimes will be here anon, and I'll hand you over to him."

The person he spoke of just then made his appearance. I did not particularly like my future commander's outside. He was a tall, gaunt man, with a long weather-beaten visage and huge black or rather grizzled whiskers ; and his voice, when he spoke, was gruff and harsh in the extreme. I need not further describe him ; only I will observe that he looked considerably cleaner then than he usually did, as I afterwards found on board the brig. He took but little notice of me beyond a slight nod, as he was busy with the ship's papers. Having pocketed them, he grasped me by the hand with a "Come along, my lad ; I am to make a seaman on ye." He spoke in a broad Northumbrian accent, and in a harsh guttural tone. I was not prepossessed in his favour, but I determined to show no signs of unwillingness to accompany him.

We were soon seated in the stern of an excessively

dirty boat, with coal-dust-begrimed rowers, who pulled away with somewhat lazy strokes towards a deeply-laden brig lying out in mid-stream. "Get on board, leddie, with you," said the captain, who had not since my first introduction addressed a single word to me. I clambered up on deck. The boat was hoisted in, the topsails let fall, and the crew, with doleful "Yeo-yo-o's," began working round the windlass, and the *Naiad* in due time was gliding down the Tyne.

She was a very different craft to what I had expected to find myself on board of. I had read about the white decks and snowy canvas, the bright polish and the active, obedient crew of a man-of-war; and such I had pictured the vessel I had hoped to sail in. The *Naiad* was certainly a contrast to this; but I kept to my resolve not to flinch from whatever turned up. When I was told to pull and haul away at the ropes, I did so with might and main; and, as everything on board was thickly coated with coal-dust, I very soon became as begrimed as the rest of the crew.

I was rather astonished, on asking Captain Grimes when tea would be ready—for I was very hungry—to be told that I might get what I could with the men forward. I went down accordingly into the forecastle, tumbling over a chest, and running my head against the stomach of one of my new shipmates as I groped my way amid the darkness which shrouded it. A cuff which sent me sprawling on the deck was the consequence. "Where are your eyes, leddie?" exclaimed a gruff voice. "Ye'll see where ye are ganging the next time."

I picked myself up, bursting into a fit of laughter, as if the affair had been a good joke. "I beg your pardon, old fellow," I said; "but if you had had a chandelier burning in this place of yours it would not have happened. How do you all manage to see down here?"

"As cats do—we're accustomed to it," said another voice; and I now began to distinguish objects around me. The watch below were seated round a sea-chest, with three or four mugs, a huge loaf of bread, and a piece of cheese and part of a flitch of fat cold bacon. It was rough fare, but I was too hungry not to be glad to partake of it.

A boy whom I had seen busy in the caboose soon came down with a kettle of hot tea. My inquiry for milk produced a general laugh, but I was told I might take as much sugar as I liked from a jar, which contained a dark-brown substance unlike any sugar I had before seen.

"Ye'll soon be asking for your bed, leddie," said Bob Tubbs, the old man whose acquaintance I had so unceremoniously formed. "Ye'll find it there, for'ard, if ye'll grope your way. It's not over airy, but it's all the warmer in winter."

After supper, I succeeded in finding the berth Bob had pointed out. It was the lowest berth, directly in the very bows of the vessel—a shelf-like space, about five feet in length, with height scarcely sufficient to allow me to sit upright,—Dirty Dick, the ship's boy I have mentioned, having the berth above me. Mine contained a mattress and a couple of blankets. My inquiry for sheets produced as much laughter as when I asked for milk. "Well, to be sure, as I suppose you have not a washerwoman on board, they would not be of much use," I sang out; "and so, unless the captain wants me to steer the ship, I will turn in and go to sleep. Good night, mates."

"The leddie has got some spirit in him," I heard

Bob Tubbs observe. "What do you call yourself, boy?"

"Happy Jack!" I sang out; "and it's not this sort of thing that's going to change me."

"You'll prove a tough one, if something else doesn't," observed Bob from his berth. "But gang to sleep, boy. Ye'll be put into a watch to-morrow, and it's the last time, may be, that ye'll have to rest through the night till ye set foot on shore again." I little then thought how long a time that would prove; but, rolling myself up in my blanket, I soon forgot where I was.

Next morning I scrambled on deck, and found the brig plunging away into a heavy sea, with a strong southerly wind, the coast just distinguishable over our starboard quarter. The captain gave me a grim smile as I made my way aft.

"Well, leddie, how do you like it?" he inquired.

"Thank you, pretty well," I answered; "but I hope we sha'n't have to wait long for breakfast."

He smiled again. "And you don't feel queer?"

"No, not a bit of it," I replied. "But I say, captain, I thought I was to come as a midshipman, and mess with the other young gentlemen on board."

He now fairly laughed outright; and looking at me for some time, answered, "We have no young gentlemen on board here. You'll get your breakfast in good time; but you are of the right sort, leddie, and little Clem shall show you what you have got to do," pointing as he spoke to a boy who just then came on deck, and whom I took to be his son.

"Thank you, captain," I observed; "I shall be glad of Clem's instruction, as I suppose he knows more about the matter than I do."

"Clem can hand, reef, and steer as well as any

one, as far as his strength goes," said the captain,
looking approvingly at him.

" I'll set to work as soon as he likes, then," I
observed. " But I wish those fellows would be sharp
about breakfast, for I am desperately hungry."

" Well, go into the cabin, and Clem will give you
a hunch of bread to stay your appetite."

I followed Clem below. " Here, Brooke, some
butter will improve it," he said, spreading a thick
slice of bread. " And so you don't seem to be sea-
sick, like most fellows. Well, I am glad of that.
My father will like you all the better for it, and soon
make a sailor of you, if you wish to learn."

I told Clem that was just what I wanted, and
that I should look to him to teach me my duties.

" I'll do my best," he said. " Take my advice and
dip your hands in the tar bucket without delay, and
don't shirk anything the mate puts you to. My
father is pretty gruff now and then, but old Growl
is a regular rough one. He does not say much to
me, but you will have to look out for squalls.
Come, we had better go on deck, or old Growl will
think that I have been putting you up to mischief.
He will soon pick a quarrel with you, to see how
you bear it."

" I'll take good care to keep out of his way, then,"
I said, bolting the last piece of bread and butter.
" Thank you, Clem, you and I shall be good friends,
I see that."

" I hope so," answered my young companion with
a sigh. " I have not many on board, and till you
came I had no one to speak to except father, and he
is not always in the mood to talk."

Clem's slice of bread and butter enabled me to
hold out till the forecastle breakfast was ready. I
did ample justice to it. Directly I made my re-ap-

pearance on deck, old Growl set me to work, and I soon had not only my hands but my arms up to the elbows in tar.   Though the vessel was pitching her head into the seas, with thick sheets of foam flying over her, he quickly sent me aloft to black down the main rigging.   Clem showed me how to secure the bucket to the shrouds while I was at work, and in spite of the violent jerks I received as the vessel plunged her bluff bows into the sea, I got on very well. · Before the evening was over I had been out on the yards with little Clem to assist in reefing the topsails, and he had shown me how to steer and box the compass.

Nothing particular occurred on the voyage, though we were ten days in reaching the mouth of the Thames.   Clem and I became great friends.   The more I saw of him the more I liked him, and wondered how so well-mannered a lad could be the son of such a man as Captain Grimes.

I saw nothing of London.   I should, indeed, have been ashamed to go on shore in my now thoroughly begrimed condition.   We were but a short time in the Thames, for as soon as we had discharged our cargo we again made sail for the Tyne.

Before this time old Growl, the mate, had taught me what starting meant.   He had generally a rope's end in his fist, and if not, one was always near at hand.   If I happened not to do a thing well enough or fast enough to please him, he was immediately after me, laying the rope across my shoulders, or anywhere he could most conveniently reach.   I generally managed to spring out of his way, and turn round and laugh at him.   If he followed me, I ran aloft, and, as I climbed much faster than he could, I invariably led him a long chase.

"I'll catch you, youngster, the next time.   Mark

me, that I will," he shouted out to me one day, when more than usually angry.

"Wait till the next time comes, mate," I sang out, and laughed more heartily than before.

The men sympathised with me, especially Dirty Dick. His shoulders, till I came on board, had been accustomed to suffer most from the mate's ill temper. Now and then old Growl, greatly to his delight, caught me unawares ; but, suffering as I did from his blows, I never let him see that I cared for them, and used to laugh just as heartily as when I had escaped from him. On this, however, he would grin sardonically, and observe, "You may laugh as you like, young master, I know what a rope's end tastes like ; it's a precious deal bitterer than you would have me fancy. I got enough of it when I was a youngster, and haven't forgotten yet."

One day when old Growl had treated me as I have described, and had gone below, Clement came up to me. "I am so sorry the mate has struck you, Brooke," he said. "It's a great shame. He dare not hit me ; and when I told father how he treats you, he told me to mind my own business, and that it was all for your good."

"I don't know how that can be," I answered ; "but I don't care for it, I can assure you. It hurts a little at the time, I'll allow, but I have got used to it, and I don't intend to let him break my spirit or make me unhappy."

Clement all the time was doing his best to teach me what he knew, and I soon learned to steer in smooth water, and could hand and reef the topsails and knot and splice as well almost as he could. Some things I did better, as I was much stronger and more active. I was put to do all sorts of unpleasant work, such as blacking down the rigging,

B

greasing the masts, and helping Dirty Dick to clean
the caboose and sweep out the forecastle. Though
I didn't like it, I went about the duty, however, as
if it was the pleasantest in the world. Pleasant or
not, I was thus rapidly becoming a seaman.

CHAPTER II.

I HAD as before, on reaching the Tyne, to remain
and keep ship, though little Clem went on shore and
did not return till we had a fresh cargo on board,
and were just about sailing.

Scarcely were we clear of the river than a heavy
gale sprang up and severely tried the old collier.
The seas came washing over her deck, and none of
us for'ard had a dry rag on our backs. When my
watch below came, I was glad to turn in between my
now darkly-tinted blankets; but they soon became
as wet as everything else, and when I went on deck
to keep my watch, I had again to put on my damp
clothes. The forecastle was fearfully hot and
steamy. We had to keep the fore hatch closed to
prevent the seas which, washing over our decks,
would otherwise have poured down upon us. In a
short time, as the ship strained more and more
while she struggled amid the waves, the water made
its way through the deck and sides till there was
not a dry space to lie on in our berths. Then I
began really to understand the miseries of forecastle
life on board a collier, and many other craft too, in
which British seamen have to sail; with bad food,
bad water, and worse treatment. Ay, I speak the
truth, which I know from experience, they have to

live like dogs, and, too often, die like dogs, with no one to care for them.

Day after day this sort of work continued. I wondered that the captain did not run back, till I heard him say that the price of coals was up in the London market, and he wanted to be there before other vessels arrived to lower it ; so, tough seaman as he was, he kept thrashing the old brig along against the south-westerly gale, which seemed to increase rather than show any signs of moderating. We had always, during each watch, to take a spell at the pumps, and now we had to keep them going without intermission. I took my turn with the rest, and my shoulders ached before I had done; still I sang and laughed away as usual.

"It's no laughing matter, youngster," said old Growl, as he passed me. "You will be laughing the wrong side of your mouth before long."

"Never fear, mate," I replied ; "both sides are the same to me."

The captain and mate at last took their turns with the rest of us, for the crew were getting worn out. I did not know the danger we were in, but I was beginning to get tired of that dreadful "clank, clank, clank."

At last, by dint of keeping at it, we had got a good way to the southward, when one night, just as we had gone about hoping to lay our course for the Thames, the wind shifted and came again right in our teeth. I had turned into my wet bunk all standing, when, having dropped off to sleep, I was awoke by a tremendous crash, and on springing up on deck I found that the mainmast had gone by the board. The gale had increased, and we were driving before it. As I made my way aft, the flashes of lightning revealed the pale faces of the

crew, some endeavouring to clear away the wreck of
the mast, others working with frantic energy at the
pumps. The leaks had increased. As may be supposed, the deeply-laden collier had but a poor chance
under such circumstances. Presently the vessel
gave a heavy lurch. A sea rolled up. The next
instant I found myself struggling in the midst of
the foaming surges. All around was dark; I felt
for the deck of the vessel, it was not beneath me; I
had been washed overboard. I struck out for life,
and in another minute I was clinging to the main-
mast, which had been cut clear. I clambered up on
it, and looked out for the brig. She was nowhere
to be seen; she must have gone down beneath the
surge which washed me from her deck. What had
become of my shipmates? I shouted again and
again at the top of my voice. There was a faint
cry, "Help me; help me." I knew the voice; it
was Clement's. Leaving the mast, I swam towards
him; he was lashed to a spar. The old captain's
last act had been to try and save the young boy's
life ere he himself sank beneath the waves. I
caught hold of the spar, bidding Clement keep his
head above the water while I towed it to the mast.
I succeeded, and then clambering on it, and casting
off the lashings, dragged him up and placed him
beside me. We hailed again and again, but no
voice replied. It may seem strange that we, the
two youngest on board, should have survived, while
all the men were drowned, but then, not one of them
could swim. We could, and, under Providence,
were able to struggle for our lives.

I did my best to cheer up little Clem, telling him
that if we could manage to hold on till daylight, as
a number of vessels were certain to pass, we should
be picked up. "I am very, very sorry, Clem, for

your father," I said; "for though he was somewhat gruff to me, he was a kind-hearted man, I am sure."

"That indeed he was," answered Clement, in a tone of sorrow. "He was always good to me; but he was not my father, as you fancy—the more reason I have to be grateful to him."

"Not your father, Clem!" I exclaimed. "I never suspected that."

"No, he was not; though he truly acted the part of one to me. Do you know, Brooke, this is not the first time that I have been left alone floating on the ocean? I was picked up by him just as you hope that we shall be picked up. I was a very little fellow, so little that I could give no account of myself. He found a black woman and me floating all alone on a raft out in the Atlantic. She died almost immediately we were rescued, without his being able to learn anything from her. He had to bury her at sea, and when he got home he in vain tried to find out my friends, though he preserved, I believe, the clothes I had on, and most of her clothes. He sent me to an excellent school, where I was well taught; and Mrs. Grimes, who was a dear, kind lady, far more refined than you would suppose his wife to have been, acted truly like a mother to me. He was very fond of her, and when she died, nearly a year ago, he took me to sea with him. I did not, however, give up my studies, but used to sit in the cabin, and every day read as much as I could. Captain Grimes used to say that he was sure I was a gentleman born, and a gentleman he wished me to be, and so I have always felt myself."

I had been struck by little Clem's refined manners, and this was now accounted for. "I am sure you are a gentleman, Clem," I observed; "and if we ever get home, my father, who is a lawyer, shall try

to find out your friends. He may be able to succeed though Captain Grimes could not. I wonder
he did not apply to my father, as, from my having
been sent on board his ship, the captain must have
known him. I suspect that they wanted to sicken
me of a sea life, and so sent me on board the *Naiad;*
but they were mistaken; and now when they hear
that she has gone down—if we are not picked up—
how sorry they will be!"

The conversation I have described was frequently
interrupted—sometimes by a heavier sea than usual
rolling by, and compelling us to hold tight for our
lives; at others we were silent for several minutes
together. We were seated on the after-part of the
maintop, the rigging which hung down on either
side acting as ballast, and contributing to keep the
wreck of the mast tolerably steady in one position.
We were thus completely out of the water, though
the spray from the crest of the seas which was blown
over us kept us thoroughly wet and cold. Fortunately, we both had on thick clothing. Clement
was always nicely dressed, for the captain, though
not particular about himself, liked to see him look
neat, while I, on the contrary, had on my oldest
working suit, and was as rough-looking a sea-dog as
could be imagined. My old tarry coat and trousers,
and sou'-wester tied under my chin, contributed,
however, to keep out the wind, and enable me the
better to endure the cold to which we were exposed.
I sheltered Clem as well as I could, and held
him tight whenever I saw a sea coming towards
him, fearing lest he might be washed away. I had
made up my mind to perish with him rather than
let him go. Hour after hour passed by, till at length,
the clouds breaking, the moon came forth and shone
down upon us. I looked at Clem's face: it was

very pale, and I was afraid he would give way altogether. "Hold on, hold on, Clem," I exclaimed. "The wind is falling, and the sea will soon go down; we shall have daylight before long, and in the meantime we have the moon to cheer us up. Perhaps we shall be on shore this time to-morrow, and comfortably in bed; and then we will go back to my father, and he will find out all about your friends. He is a wonderfully clever man, though a bit strict, to be sure."

"Thank you, Jack, thank you," he answered. "Don't be afraid; I feel pretty strong, only somewhat cold and hungry."

Just then I recollected that I had put the best part of a biscuit into my pocket at tea-time, having been summoned on deck as I was eating it. It was wet, to be sure; but such biscuits as we had take a good deal of soaking to soften thoroughly. I felt for it. There it was. So I put a small piece into Clem's mouth. He was able to swallow it. Then I put in another, and another; and so I fed him, till he declared he felt much better. I had reserved a small portion for myself, but as I knew that I could go on without it, I determined to keep it, lest he should require more.

I continued to do my best to cheer him up by talking to him of my home, and how he might find his relations and friends, and then I bethought me that I would sing a song. I don't suppose that many people have sung under such circumstances, but I managed to strike up a stave, one of those with which I had been accustomed to amuse my messmates in the *Naiad's* forecastle. It was not, perhaps, one of the merriest, but it served to divert Clem's thoughts, as well as mine, from our perilous position.

" I wish that I could sing too," said Clem ; "but I know I could not, if I was to try. I wonder you can, Jack."

"Why ? because I am sure that we shall be picked up before long, and so I see no reason why I should not try to be happy," I answered thoughtlessly.

"Ah, but I am thinking of those who are gone," said Clem. "My kind father, as I called him, and old Growl, and the rest of the poor fellows; it is like singing over their graves."

"You are right, Clem," I said ; "I will sing no more, though I only did it to keep up your spirits. But what is that ?" I exclaimed, suddenly, as we rose to the crest of a sea. "A large ship standing directly for us."

"Yes ; she is close-hauled, beating down Channel," observed Clement. "She will be right upon us, too, if she keeps her present course."

"We must take care to let her know where we are, by shouting together at the top of our voices when we are near enough to be heard," I said.

" She appears to me to be a man-of-war, and probably a sharp look-out is kept forward," Clement remarked. We had not observed the ship before, as our faces had been turned away from her. The sea had, however, been gradually working the mast round, as I knew to be the case by the different position in which the moon appeared to us.

" We must get ready for a shout, Clem, and then cry out together as we have never cried before. I'll say when we are to begin."

As the ship drew nearer Clem had no doubt that she was a man-of-war, a large frigate apparently, under her three topsails and courses.

" She is passing to windward of us," I exclaimed.

"Not so sure of that," cried Clem. "She will be right over us if we do not cry out in time."

"Let us begin, then," I said. "Now, shout away, Hip! Hip!"

"No, no!" cried Clem, "that will not do. Shout 'Ship ahoy!'"

I had forgotten for the moment what to say, so together we began shouting as shrilly as we could, at the very top of our voices. Again and again we shouted. I began to fear that the ship would be right over us, when presently we saw her luff up. The moon was shining down upon us, and we were seen. So close, even then, did the frigate pass, that the end of the mast we were clinging to almost grazed her side. Ropes were hove to us, but the ship had too much way on her, and it was fortunate we could not seize them. "Thank you," I cried out. "Will you take us aboard?" There was no answer, and I thought that we were to be left floating on our mast till some other vessel might sight us. We were mistaken, though. We could hear loud orders issued on board, but what was said we could not make out, and presently the ship came up to the wind, the head yards were braced round, and she lay hove to. Then we saw a boat lowered. How eagerly we watched what was being done. She came towards us. The people in her shouted to us in a strange language. They were afraid, evidently, of having their boat stove in by the wreck of the mast. At last they approached us cautiously.

"Come, Clem, we will swim to her," I said. "Catch tight hold of my jacket; I have got strength enough left in me for that."

We had not far to go, but I found it a tougher job than I expected. It would have been wiser to have remained till we could have leaped from the

mast to the boat. I was almost exhausted by the
time we reached her, and thankful when I felt Clem
lifted off my back, I myself, when nearly sinking,
being next hauled on board. We were handed into
the stern sheets, where we lay almost helpless. I
tried to speak, but could not, nor could I understand
a word that was said. The men at once pulled back
to the ship, and a big seaman, taking Clem under
one of his arms, clambered up with him on deck.
Another carried me on board in the same fashion.
The boat was then hoisted up, and the head yards
being braced round, the ship continued her course.
Lanterns being brought, we were surrounded by a
group of foreign-looking seamen, who stared curiously
at us, asking, I judged from the tones of their voices,
all sorts of questions, but as their language was as
strange to us as ours was to them, we couldn't
understand a word they said, or make them comprehend what we said.

"If you would give us some hot grog, and let us
turn into dry hammocks, we should be much obliged
to you," I cried out at last, despairing of any good
coming of all their talking.

Just as I spoke, an officer with a cloak on came
from below, having apparently turned out of his
berth. "Ah, you are English," I heard him say.
"Speak to me. How came you floating out
here?"

I told him that our vessel had gone down, and
that we, as far as I knew, were the only survivors of
the crew.

"And who is that other boy?"

"The captain's son," I answered.

"Ah, I thought so, by his appearance," said the
officer. "He shall be taken into the cabin. You,
my boy, will have a hammock on the lower deck,

and the hot grog you asked for. I'll visit you soon.
I am the doctor of the ship."

He then spoke to the men, and while Clement
was carried aft, I was lifted up and conveyed below
by a couple of somewhat rough but not ill-natured-
looking seamen. I was more exhausted than I had
supposed, for on the way I fainted, and many hours
passed by before I returned to a state of half consciousness.

CHAPTER III.

IN three days I was quite well, and the doctor
sending me a suit of seaman's clothes, I dressed
and found my way up on deck. I looked about
eagerly for Clem, but not seeing him, I became
anxious to learn how he was. I could make none
of the men understand me. Most of them were
Finns—big broad-shouldered, ruddy, light haired,
bearded fellows ; very good-natured and merry,
notwithstanding the harsh treatment they often
received. Big as they were, they were knocked
about like so many boys by the petty officers, and
I began to feel rather uncomfortable lest I should
come in for share of the same treatment, of which I
had had enough from the hands of old Growl. I
determined, however, to grin and bear it, and do, as
well as I could, whatever I was told.

I soon found that I was not to be allowed to eat
the bread of idleness, for a burly officer, whom I
took to be the boatswain, ordered me aloft with
several other boys, to hand the fore royal, a stiff
breeze just then coming on. Up I went ; and

though I had never been so high above the deck before, that made but little difference, and I showed that I could beat my companions in activity. When I came down the boatswain nodded his approval. I kept looking out for Clem. At last I saw my friend the doctor, with several other officers, on the quarter-deck. I hurried aft to him, and, touching my cap, asked him how Clem was. The others stared at me as if surprised at my audacity in thus venturing among them. "The boy is doing well," he answered; "but, lad, I must advise you not to infringe the rules of discipline. You were, I understand, one of the ship's boys, and must remain for'ard. He is a young gentleman, and such his dress and appearance prove him to be, will be allowed to live with the midshipmen." "I am very glad to hear that," I answered; "but I am a gentleman's son also, and I should like to live with the midshipmen, that I may be with Clem." "Your companion has said something to the same effect," observed the doctor; "but the captain remarks that there are many wild, idle boys sent to sea who may claim to be the sons of gentlemen; and as your appearance shows, as you acknowledge was the case, that you were before the mast, there you must continue till your conduct proves that you are deserving of a higher rank. And now go for'ard. I'll recollect what you have said." I took the hint. The seamen grinned as I returned among them, as if they had understood what I had been saying.

I kept to my resolution of doing smartly whatever I was told, and laughed and joked with the men, trying to understand their lingo, and to make myself understood by them. I managed to pick up some of their words, though they almost cracked my jaws to pronounce them; but I laughed at my own mistakes, and they seemed to think it very good fun to hear me talk.

Several days passed away, when at length I saw Clement come on deck. I ran aft to him, and he came somewhat timidly to meet me. We shook hands, and I told him how glad I was to see him better, though he still looked very pale. "I am very glad also to see you, Jack," he said, "and I wish we were to be together. I told the doctor I would rather go and live for'ard than be separated from you; but he replied that that could not be, and I have hopes, Jack, that by-and-by you will be placed on the quarter-deck if you will enter the Russian service." "What! and give up being an Englishman?" I exclaimed. "I would do a great deal to be with you, but I won't abandon my country and be transmogrified into a Russian." "You are right, Jack," said Clem, with a sigh; "however, the officers will not object to my talking with you, and we must hope for the best." After this I was constantly thinking how I should act should I have the option of being placed on the quarter-deck and becoming an officer in the Russian service, for we were on board a Russian frigate.

Clem got rapidly better, and we every day met and had a talk together. Altogether, as the boatswain's lash did not often reach me, though he used it pretty freely among my companions, I was as happy as usual. I should have been glad to have had less train-oil and fat in the food served out to us, and should have preferred wheaten flour to the black rye and beans which I had to eat. Still that was a trifle, and I soon got accustomed to the greasy fare. Clem was now doing duty as a midshipman, and I was in the same watch with him.

The weather had hitherto been generally fine;

but one night as the sun went down, I thought I
saw indications of a gale. Still the wind didn't
come, and the ship went gliding smoothly over the
ocean. I was in the middle watch, and had just
come on deck. I had made my way aft, where I
found Clem, and, leaning against a gun, we were
talking together of dear old England, wondering
when we should get back there, when a sudden
squall struck the ship, and the hands were ordered
aloft to reef topsails. I sprang aloft with the rest,
and lay out on the lee fore yard-arm. I was so
much more active than most of my shipmates, that
I had become somewhat careless. As I was leaning
over to catch hold of a reef point, I lost my balance,
and felt, as I fell head foremost, that I was about to
have my brains dashed out on the deck below me.
The instant before the wind had suddenly ceased,
and the sail giving a flap, hung down almost against
the mast. Just at that moment, filled with the
breeze, it bulged out again, and striking me, sent
me flying overboard. Instinctively I put my hands
together, and, plunging down, struck the now foaming water head first. I sank several feet, though I
scarcely for a moment lost consciousness, and when
I came to the surface I found myself striking out
away from the ship, which was gliding rapidly by
me. I heard a voice sing out, "A man overboard."
I knew that it must have been Clem's, and I saw a
spar and several other things thrown into the water.
I do not know whether the life-buoy was let go. I
did not see it. Turning round I struck out in
the wake of the ship, but the gale just then coming
with tremendous fury, drove her on fast away from
me, and she speedily disappeared in the thick
gloom. I should have lost all hope had I not at
that moment come against a spar, and a large

basket with·a rope attached to it, which was driven almost into my hands. Climbing on to the spar, to which I managed to lash the basket, I then got into the latter, where I could sit without much risk of being washed out. It served, indeed, as a tolerably efficient life-preserver; for although the water washed in and washed out, and the seas frequently broke over my head, I was able to hold myself in without much trouble. I still had some hopes that the ship would come back and look for me.

At length I thought I saw her approaching through the darkness. It raised my spirits, and I felt a curious satisfaction, in addition to the expectation of being saved, at the thought that I was not to be carelessly abandoned to my fate. I anxiously gazed in the direction where I fancied the ship to be, but she drew no nearer, and the dark void filled the space before me. Still I did not give way to despair, though I found it a hard matter to keep up. I had been rescued before, and I hoped to be saved another time. Then, however, I had been in a comparatively narrow sea, with numerous vessels passing over it. Now I was in the middle of the Atlantic, which, although rightly called a highway, was a very broad one. I could not also help recollecting that I was in the latitude where sharks abound, and I thought it possible that one might make a grab at my basket, and try to swallow it and me together, although I smiled at the thought of the inconvenience the fish would feel when it stuck its teeth into the yard, and got it fixed across its mouth. Happily no shark espied me.

Day at last dawned. As I looked around when I rose to the summit of a sea, my eyes fell alone on the dark, tumbling, foaming waters, and the thick

clouds going down to meet them. I began to feel
very hungry and thirsty, for though I had water
enough around me, I dare not drink it. I now
found it harder than ever to keep up my spirits, and
gloomy thoughts began to take possession of my
mind. No one, I confess, would have called me
Happy Jack just then. I was sinking off into a
state of stupor, during which I might easily have
been washed out of my cradle, when, happening to
open my eyes, they fell on the sails of a large brig
standing directly for me. I could scarcely fail to
be seen by those on board. On she came before the
breeze ; but as she drew nearer I began to fear that
she might still pass at some distance. I tried to
stand up and shout out, but I was nearly toppling
overboard in making the attempt. I managed, however, to kneel upon the spar and wave my handker-
chief, shouting as I did so with all my might. The
brig altered her course, and now came directly down
for me. I made out two or three people in the fore-
chains standing ready to heave me a rope. I prepared to seize it. The brig was up to me and nearly
running me down, but I caught the first rope hove
to me, and grasped it tightly. I could scarcely have
expected to find myself capable of so much exertion.
Friendly hands were stretched out to help me up,
but scarcely was I safe than I sank down almost
senseless on deck. I soon, however, recovered, and
being taken below, and dry clothes and food being
given me, I quickly felt as well as usual. " Where
am I, and where are you bound to ?" were the first
questions I asked, hoping to hear that I was on
board a homeward-bound vessel. " You are on
board the American brig *Fox* bound out round
the Horn to the Sandwich Islands and the west
coast of North America," was the answer. " But I

want to go home to England," I exclaimed. "Well,
then, I guess you had better get into your basket,
and wait till another vessel picks you up," replied
the captain, to whom I had addressed myself.
"Thank you, I would rather stay here with dry
clothes on my back and something to eat," I said.
"Perhaps, however, captain, you will speak any
homeward-bound vessel we meet, and get her to take
me?" "Not likely to fall in with one," he observed.
"You had better make the best of things where you
are." "That's what I always try to do," I replied.
"You are the right sort of youngster for me, then,"
he said. "Only don't go boasting of your proud
little venomous island among my people. We are
true Americans, fore and aft, except some of the
passengers, and they would be better off if they
would sink their notions and pay more respect to
the stars and stripes. However, you will have
nothing to do with them, for you will do your duty
for'ard I guess." I thought it wiser to make no
reply to these remarks, and as the crew were just
going to dinner, I gladly accompanied them into
their berth under the top-gallant forecastle. The
crew, I found, though American citizens, were of all
nationalities—Danes, and Swedes, and Frenchmen,
with too or three mulattoes and a black cook. They
described Captain Pyke, for that was the master's
name, as a regular Tartar, and seemed to have no
great love for him, though they held him in especial
awe. I was thankful at being so soon picked up,
but I would rather have found myself on board a
different style of craft. The cabin passengers were
going out to join one of the establishments of the
great Fur Trading Company on the Columbia river.
They were pleasant, gentlemanly-looking men, and
I longed to introduce myself to them, as I was

beginning to get somewhat **weary of the rough**
characters with whom I was doomed to associate.
But from what the men told me, I felt sure that if
I did so I should make the captain my enemy. He
and they were evidently not on good terms. I got
on, however, pretty well with the crew, and as I
could speak a little French, I used to talk to the
Frenchmen in their own language, my mistakes
affording them considerable amusement, though, as
they corrected me, I gradually improved.

Among the crew were two other persons whom I
will particularly mention. One went by the name
of "Old Tom." He was relatively old with regard to
the rest of our shipmates, rather than old in years—
a wiry, active, somewhat wizen-faced man, with
broad shoulders, and possessing great muscular
strength. I suspected from the first, from the way
he spoke, that he was not a Yankee born. His
language, when talking to me, was always correct,
without any nasal twang; and that he was a man of
some education I was convinced, when I heard him
once quote, as if speaking to himself, a line of
Horace. He never smiled, and there was a melancholy expression on his countenance, which made me
fancy that something weighed on his mind. He did
not touch spirits, but his short pipe was seldom out
of his mouth. When, however, he sat with the rest
in the forecastle berth, his manner completely
changed, and he talked, and argued, and wrangled,
and guessed, and calculated, with as much vehe-
mence as any one, entering with apparent zest into
their ribald conversation, though even then the most
humorous remark or jest failed to draw forth a laugh
from his lips.

CHAPTER IV.

THE other person was a lad a couple of years my senior, called always "Young Sam," apparently one of those unhappy waifs cast on the bleak world without relations or friends to care for him. He was a fine young fellow, with a blue laughing eye, dauntless and active, and promised to become a good seaman. In spite of the rough treatment he often received from his shipmates, he kept up his spirits, and as our natures in that respect assimilated, I felt drawn towards him. The only person who seemed to take any interest in him, however, was old Tom, who saved him from many a blow; still, no two characters could apparently have more completely differed. Young Sam seemed a thoughtless, care-for-nothing fellow, always laughing and jibing those who attacked him, and ready for any fun or frolic which turned up. He appreciated, however, old Tom's kindness; and the only times I saw him look serious were when he received a gentle rebuke from his friend for any folly he had committed which had brought him into trouble. I believe, indeed, that young Sam would have gone through fire and water to show his gratitude to old Tom, while I suspect that the latter, in spite of his harsh exterior, had a heart not altogether seared by the world, which required some one on whom to fix its kindlier feelings.

I had been some time on board when we put into a port at the Falkland Islands, then uninhabited, to obtain a supply of water. While the crew of the boats were engaged in filling the casks, Mr. Duncan, one of the gentlemen, taking young Sam with him, went into the interior to shoot wild-fowl.

The casks were filled; and the boats, after waiting for some time the return of Mr. Duncan and Sam, came back. Mr. Symonds, the second mate, proposed to return for our shipmates after the casks had been hoisted on board. The captain seemed very angry at this ; and when Mr. Symonds was shoving off from the brig's side, ordered him back. He was hesitating, when another gentleman jumped into the boat, declaring that he would not allow his companion to be left behind, and promised the men a reward if they would shove off. Two of the men agreed to go in the boat, and the mate, with the rest, coming up the side, they pulled away for the shore.

The captain walked the deck, fuming and raging, every now and then turning an angry glance at the land and pulling out his watch. "He means mischief," muttered old Tom in my hearing ; "but if he thinks to leave young Sam ashore to die of starvation, he is mistaken."

The night drew on, and the boat had not returned. My watch being over, I turned in, supposing that the brig would remain at anchor till the morning. I was, however, awakened in the middle watch by old Tom's voice. "Come on deck, Jack," he said ; "there's mischief brewing ; the captain had a quarrel with Mr. Duncan the other day, and he hates young Sam for his impudence, as he calls it, and so I believe he intends to leave them behind if he can do so ; but he is mistaken. We will not lift anchor till they are safe on board, or a party has been sent to look for them. They probably lost their way, and could not get back to the harbour before dark. There are no wild beasts or savages on shore, and so they could not come to harm ; you slip into the cabin, and call the other gentlemen, and I'll manage the crew, who have just loosed topsails, and are already at the windlass with the cable hove short."

I was on deck in an instant, and, keeping on one side, while the captain was on the other, managed to slip into the cabin. I told the gentlemen of old Tom's suspicions, and observed that the captain probably thought those in the boat would return without Mr. Duncan and Sam, when they saw the vessel making sail.

They instantly began to dress; and one of them, a spirited young Highlander, Mr. M'Ivor, put a brace of pistols into his belt and followed me on deck. I tried to escape being seen by the captain, but he caught sight of me, I was sure, though I stooped down and kept close to the bulwarks as I crept for'ard.

By this time the men were heaving at the windlass, which they continued to do, in spite of what old Tom said to them. The captain had overheard him, and threatened to knock the first man down with a handspike who ceased to work. Old Tom, however, had got one in his hand, and the captain did not dare to touch him. In another instant I heard Mr. M'Ivor's voice exclaiming, "What is this all about, Captain Pyke? What! are you going to leave our friends on shore?" "If your friends don't come off at the proper time they must take the consequences," answered the captain. "Then, what I have got to say, Captain Pyke, is, that I'll not allow them to be deserted, and that I intend to carry out my resolution with a pretty strong argument— the instant the anchor leaves the ground I'll shoot you through the head." "Mutiny! mutiny!" shouted the captain, starting back, "seize this man and heave him overboard." As he spoke the other two gentlemen made their appearance, and old Tom and I, with two or three others, stepped up close to them, showing the captain the side we intended to take. Neither of the mates moved, while the men folded their arms and looked on, showing that they did not intend to interfere.

"Very well, gentlemen," cried the captain, "I see how matters stand—you have been bribing the crew. I'll agree to wait for the boat, and if she does not come with the missing people we must give them up for lost." "That depends upon circumstances," said Mr. M'Ivor, returning his pistol to his belt. He and the rest continued to walk the deck, while the captain went, muttering threats of vengeance, into his cabin.

None of us after this turned in. In a short time the splash of oars was heard, and the boat came alongside. "We have come for food," said Mr. Fraser, one of the gentlemen who had gone in her. "I intend going back at daylight, and must get two or three others to accompany me. We will then have a thorough search for Duncan and the boy— there is no doubt that they have lost their way, and if we fire a few muskets, they will, with the help of daylight, easily find the harbour. Mr. M'Ivor promised to accompany his friend, and I volunteered to go also." "No, Jack," said old Tom, "you remain with me. If we all go, the captain may be playing us some trick." I don't know what side old Tom would have taken if it had not been for young Sam. Judging by his usual conduct, I suspect that he would have stood with his arms folded, and let the rest, as he would have said, fight it out by themselves.

At daylight the boat pulled away with Mr. M'Ivor and another additional hand, taking a couple of muskets with them. Shortly afterwards the captain appeared on deck—though he cast frequent angry glances towards the shore, he said nothing—probably he could not afford to lose so many hands, as

there were now four away, besides the two gentlemen, while the aspect of old Tom, with the rest of
the crew, kept him from attempting to carry out his
evil intentions. Two or three times, notwithstanding this, I thought he was about to order the anchor
to be hove up ; but again he seemed to hesitate,
and at length, towards noon, the boat was seen
coming off, with Mr. Duncan and Sam in her. The
captain said nothing to the gentlemen, but, as soon
as the boat was hoisted up, he began to belabour
poor Sam with a rope's end. He was still striking
the lad, when old Tom stepped between them,
grasping a handspike. " What has the lad done,
sir ?" he exclaimed. " Why not attack Mr. Duncan ?
If anyone is to blame for the delay, he is the person,
not young Sam." The gentlemen were advancing
while old Tom was speaking, and several of the crew
cried out shame. The captain again found himself
in the minority, and, without replying to old Tom,
walked aft, muttering between his teeth.

These incidents will give some idea of the state of
matters on board the ship.

We now made sail, with a gentle breeze right aft,
but scarcely had we lost sight of the islands when a
heavy gale sprang up. The lighter canvas was instantly handed—young Sam and one of the men
who had gone in the boat were ordered out on the
jibboom to furl the flying jib. As they were about
this work, a tremendous sea struck the bows, the
gaskets got loose, the jibboom was carried away, and
with it the two poor fellows who were endeavouring
to secure the sail. The captain, who had seen the
accident, took no notice of it, but the first mate, not
wishing to have their death on his conscience,
sprang aft and ordered the ship to be brought to,
while others hove overboard every loose piece of

timber, empty casks, or hencoops, which they could lay hands on, to give our shipmates a chance of escape. Old Tom and I instantly ran to the jolly-boat, and were easing off the falls, when I felt my-self felled to the deck by a blow on the head, the captain's voice exclaiming, "What, you fools, do you wish to go after them and be drowned too?" When I came to myself I saw the boat made fast, and could just distinguish the articles thrown over-board floating astern, while old Tom was standing gazing at them with sorrowful looks, the eyes of all on board, indeed, being turned in the same direction.

"It would have been no use, Jack," he said, heaving a deep sigh; "the captain was right, the boat couldn't have lived two minutes in this sea, but I would have risked my life to try and save young Sam, though, for your sake, my boy, it's better as it is."

After this the ship was put on her course, and we stood on, plunging away into the heavy seas which rose around us, and threatened every instant to break on board the brig. The passengers looked, and, I daresay, felt very melancholy at the accident, for young Sam especially, was liked by them, and on that account Mr. Duncan had taken him on his ex-pedition. Old Tom could scarcely lift up his head, and even the rest of the crew refrained from their usual gibes and jokes. The captain said nothing, but I saw by the way he treated the first mate that he was very savage with him for the part he had taken in attempting to save the poor fellows.

After this old Tom was kinder than ever to me, and evidently felt towards me as he had towards young Sam, whose duties as everybody's servant I had now to take, being the youngest on board, and least able to hold my own against the captain's

tyranny, and the careless and often rough treatment
of the crew.

I had some time before told poor young Sam how
I used to be called "Happy Jack," and he went and
let out what I had said among the men. When one
of them started me with a rope's end, he would sing
out, "That's for you, 'Happy Jack.'" Another
would exclaim, "Go and swab the deck down,
'Happy Jack;'" or, "'Happy Jack,' go and help
Mungo to clean out the caboose, I hope you are
happy now—pleasant work for a young gentleman,
isn't it?" "Look you," I replied one day, when this
remark was made to me, " I am alive and well, and
hope some day to see my home and friends, so, com-
pared to the lot of poor young Sam and Dick
Noland, who are fathoms deep down in the ocean, I
think I have a right to say I am happy—your kicks
and cuffs only hurt for a time, and I manage
soon to forget them. If it's any pleasure to you to
give them, all I can say is, that it's a very rum sort
of pleasure; and now you have got my opinion about
the matter."

"That's the spirit I like to see," exclaimed old
Tom, slapping me on the back soon afterwards,
"You'll soon put a stop to that sort of thing." I
found he was right; and, though I had plenty of
dirty work to do, still, after that, not one of the men
ever lifted his hand against me. The captain, however, was not to be so easily conquered, and so I
took good care to stand clear of him whenever I
could.

The rough weather continued till we had made
Cape Horn, which rose dark and frowning out of
the wild heaving ocean. We were some time
doubling it, and were several days in sight of Terra
del Fuego, but we did not see anything like a

burning mountain—indeed, no volcanoes exist at that end of the Andes.

The weather moderated soon after we were round the Horn, but in a short time another gale sprung up, during which our bulwarks were battered in, one of our boats carried away, our bowsprit sprung, and the foretop-sail, the only canvas we had set, blown to ribbons. Besides this, we received other damages, which contributed still further to sour our captain's temper. We were at one time so near the iron-bound coast that there seemed every probability that we should finish off by being dashed to pieces on the rocks. Happily, the wind moderated, and a fine breeze springing up, we ran on merrily into the Pacific.

Shortly after, we made the island of Juan Fernandez, and, as I saw its wood-covered heights rising out of the blue ocean, I could not help longing to go on shore and visit the scenes I had read about in Robinson Crusoe. I told old Tom about my wish. Something more like a smile than I had ever yet seen, rose on his countenance. " I doubt, Jack, that you would find any traces of the hero you are so fond of," he observed; " I believe once upon a time an Englishman did live there, left by one of the ships of Commodore Anson's squadron, but that was long ago, and the Spaniards have turned it into a prison, something like our Norfolk Island."

CHAPTER V.

WE, however, did call off another island in the neighbourhood, called Massafuera, to obtain a supply of wood and water. The ship was hove-to, and the pinnace and jolly-boat were sent on shore with casks. I was anxious to go, but old Tom kept me back. "You stay where you are, Jack," he said, "or the skipper may play you some trick. It's a dangerous place to land at, you are sure of a wetting, and may lose your life in going through the surf."

In the evening, when the party returned, I found this to be the case. Still, I might have been tempted, I think, to run off and let the ship sail away without me, as I heard that there were plenty of goats on the island, abundance of water, and that the vegetation was very rich.

It is also an exceedingly picturesque spot, the mountains rising abruptly from the sea, surrounded by a narrow strip of beach. Those who went on shore had also caught a large quantity of fish, of various sorts, as well as lobsters and crabs, which supplied all hands for several days.

Perhaps old Tom had a suspicion of what I might have been tempted to do, and I fancied that was his chief reason for keeping me on board.

The idea having once taken possession of my mind, I resolved to make my escape at the next tempting-looking island we might touch at, should I find any civilized men living there, or should it be uninhabited. I had no wish to live among savages, as I had read enough of their doings to make me anxious to keep out of their way, and I was not influenced by motives which induce seamen to run from their ships for the sake of living an idle, profligate life, free from the restraints of civilization.

A few days after leaving Massafuera, we got into the trade winds, which carried us swiftly along to the northward. Again we crossed the equator; and about three weeks afterwards made the island of Owhyee, the largest of the Sandwich

Islands.   As we coasted along, we enjoyed the most magnificent view I had ever beheld.   Along the picturesque shore were numerous beautiful plantations, while beyond it rose the rocky and dreary sides of the gigantic Mouna Roa, its snow-clad summit towering to the clouds.   It was on this island that Captain Cook was murdered by the now friendly and almost civilized natives, who have, indeed, since become in many respects completely so, and taken their place among the nations of the world.

We sailed on, passing several islands, when we brought up in the beautiful bay of Whytetee.   Near the shore was a village situated in an open grove of cocoa-nut trees, with the hills rising gently in the rear, presenting a charming prospect.   The more I gazed at it, the more I longed to leave the brig, and go and dwell there, especially as I heard that there were several respectable Englishmen and Americans already settled on the island, and that they were held in high favour by the king and his chiefs.   Still old Tom had been so kind to me, and I entertained so sincere a regard for him, that I could not bear the thoughts of going away without bidding him farewell.   I was afraid, however, of letting him know my intentions.   Often I thought that I would try and persuade him to go too.   I began by speaking of the beautiful country, and the delicious climate, and the kind manners of the people, and how pleasantly our countrymen, residing there, must pass their lives.   "I know what you are driving at, Jack," he said, "You want to run from the ship; isn't it so?"   I confessed that such was the case, and asked him to go with me.   "No, Jack," he replied, "I am not one of those fellows who act thus; I have done many a thing I am sorry for, but I engaged for the voyage, and swore to stick by the brig; and while she holds together, unless the captain sets me free, I intend to do so. And Jack, though you are at liberty to do what you like, you wouldn't leave me, would you?" He spoke with much feeling in his tone. "Since young Sam went, you are the only person I have cared to speak to on board, and if you were to go, I should feel as if I were left alone in the world. I should have liked to have made friends with those fine young men, Duncan and M'Ivor. Once (you may be surprised to hear it) I was their equal in position, but they don't trouble themselves about such a man as I now am, and they will soon be leaving the brig for the shore. If I thought it was for your advantage, I would say, notwithstanding this, go; but it isn't. You will get into bad ways if you go and live among those savages—for savages they are, whatever you may say about them. And you will probably be able to return home by sticking to the brig sooner than any other way."

These arguments weighed greatly with me, and I finally abandoned my intention, greatly to old Tom's satisfaction. He redoubled his kindness to me after this. Towards every one else he grew more silent and reserved.

I may just say, that the next day we anchored off Honoluloo, the chief town, where the king and his court resided; and that we carried on some trading with the people, his majesty in particular, and taking some half-a-dozen Sandwich islanders on board to replace the men we had lost, and, as old Tom observed, any others we might lose, we sailed for the American coast.

From that day I could not help observing a more than usually sad expression on my friend's countenance; indeed, every day he seemed to become more and more gloomy, and I determined to ask him what there was on his mind to make him so. I took the opportunity I was looking for one night when he was at the helm, and the second mate, who was officer of the watch, had gone forward to have a chat, as he sometimes did, with the men. The night was fine and clear, and we were not likely to have eaves-droppers. "Tell me, Tom," I said, "what is the matter with you? I wish that I could be of as much use to you as you have been to me." "Thank you, Jack," he answered; "the fact is, I have got something on my mind, and as you have given me an opportunity, I'll tell you what it is. I think I shall be the better afterwards, and you may be able to do for me what I shall never have an opportunity of doing myself, for, Jack, I cannot help feeling sure that my days are numbered. If that captain of ours wishes to get rid of me, he will find means without staining his hands in my blood, he will not do that, there are plenty of other ways by which I may be expended, as they say of old stores in the navy. For myself I care but little, but I should wish to remain to look after you, and lend you a helping hand should you need it." "Thank you, Tom," I said, "I value the kind feelings you entertain for me, and I hope that we shall be together till we reach England again. But I was going to ask why you think that the captain wishes to get rid of you? He can have no motive that I can discover to desire your death."

"He hates me, that's enough; he's a man who will go any lengths to gratify his hate," answered old Tom. "But I promised to tell you about the matter which weighs on my mind. Jack, I did many things when I was a young man, which I am sorry for, but I was then chiefly my own enemy. A time came, however, when I was tempted to commit a crime against others, and it's only since I began this voyage that I have had a wish to try and undo it as far as I have the power. You must know, Jack, I am the son of a gentleman, and I went to college. I had got into bad ways there, and spent all my property. When my last shilling was gone, I shipped on board a merchant vessel, and for years never again set foot on the shores of old England. I knocked about all that time in different climes and vessels, herding with the roughest and most abandoned class of seamen, till I became almost as abandoned and rough as they were. Still, during all my wanderings, I had a hankering for the associates and the refinements of society I had so long quitted. Thoughts of home would come back to me even in my wildest moments, although I tried hard to keep them out. At length I returned to England with more money in my pocket than I had ever again expected to possess. Throwing aside my seafaring clothes as soon as I got on shore, I dressed myself as a gentleman, and repairing to a fashionable watering-place, where I found several old friends, managed to get into respectable society. I forgot that unless I could obtain some employment my money must soon come to an end. It did so, but the taste for good society had been revived in me. It was now impossible to indulge in it, and I was compelled once more to seek for a berth on board ship. Thoughtlessly, I had never studied navigation while I was at sea, and consequently had again to go before the mast. I got on board an Indiaman, and reached Calcutta. On the return voyage we had a number of passengers. I of course knew but little about them, as I seldom went aft except to take my trick at the helm. I observed, however, among them a gentle-

D

man of refined appearance, with his wife and their little boy. They had a native nurse to take care of him. No one could be more affectionate than the gentleman was to his wife and child, but he seemed of a retiring disposition, and I seldom saw him speaking to any one else. We had had particularly fine weather during the greater part of the passage, when the ship was caught in a tremendous gale. During it the masts were carried away, several of the hands—Lascars and Englishmen—were lost overboard, while she sprung a leak, which kept all the crew hard at work at the pumps.

" It became evident, indeed, before long, that unless the weather moderated the ship would go down. We had four boats remaining, but as they would not carry a third of the people on board, the captain ordered all hands to turn to and build rafts. We were thus employed when night came on; such a night I never before had seen. The thunder roared and the lightning flashed around us, as if it would set the ship on fire. Some hours passed away; we could get on but slowly with our work. I was on the after-part of the deck, when I remember seeing the gentleman I have spoken of come up and make an offer to the captain to lend a hand at whatever might be required to be done. I observed at the time that he had a small case hanging to his side. He did not seem to think that there was any danger of the ship going down for many hours to come; nor indeed did any one; for the leaks were gaining but little on the pumps, although they were gaining. He seemed so well to understand what he was about that I suspected he was a naval officer. We worked away hard, and it was nearly morning, when a dreadful peal of thunder, such as I had never heard before, broke over our heads, and it's my belief that a bolt passed right through the ship. Be that as it may, a fearful cry arose that she was going down. The people rushed to the boats. Discipline was at an end. The gentleman I spoke of shouted to the men, trying to bring them back to their duty. Then I saw him, when all hope of doing so had gone, hurry into the cuddy. Directly afterwards he came out with his wife and child, together with the nurse. Supposing, I fancy, that the boats were already full, or would be swamped alongside, he secured the nurse to the raft we had been building, and had given her the child to hold, calling on me and others to assist in launching it overboard, intending to take his place with his wife upon it. He was in the act of securing her—so it seemed to me—when the ship gave a fearful plunge forward, and a roaring sea swept over her. I at once saw that she would never rise again. On came the foaming waters, carrying all before them. Whether or not the gentleman and his wife succeeded in getting to the raft, I could not tell; there was no room, I knew, for me on it. Just before I had caught sight of one of the boats, which had shoved off with comparatively few people in her, dropping close under the ship's quarter. I sprang aft, and, leaping overboard, struck out towards her, managing to get hold of her bow as it dipped into the sea. I hauled myself on board. By the time I had got in, and could look about me, I saw the stern of the ship sinking beneath a wave, and for a moment I thought the boat would have been drawn down with her. Such fearful shrieks and cries as I never wish to hear again rose from amid the foaming sea, followed by a perfect and scarcely less terrible silence. We had but three oars in the boat, which we could with difficulty, therefore, manage in that heavy sea. Most of the men in her were Lascars, and they were but little disposed to go to the assistance of our drowning shipmates. There were three Englishmen in the after-part of the boat, and I made my way among the Lascars to join them. Even the Englishmen belonged to the least respectable part of the crew. They, however, sided with me, and, seizing a stretcher, I swore that I would brain the fellows if they would not try to pick up some of the drowning people. Two or three on this drew their knives, flourishing them with threatening gestures. Knowing them pretty well, I felt sure that if we did not gain the day, they would take the first opportunity of heaving us overboard; and with all my might I dealt a blow at the head of the man nearest me, who held his weapon ready to strike. The stretcher caught him as he was in the act of springing up, and he fell overboard, sinking immediately. "Any more of you like to be treated in the same way?" I exclaimed. The wretches sank down in their seats, thoroughly cowed; but in the scuffle one of the oars was lost overboard, and was swept away before we could recover it. Some time was thus lost, and the boat had drifted a considerable distance from the spot where the Indiaman had gone down. We could hear, however, cries for help rising above the hissing and dashing sounds of the tumbling waters. Every instant I expected that the boat would be swamped; when at length the Lascars, who had the oars, were induced by my threats to pull away and keep her head to sea. I had taken the helm, and though we made no progress, the rafts and various articles which had floated up from the wreck came drifting down towards us, scattering far and wide over the tossing ocean. I caught sight of a boat and two or three other rafts, but they were too far off to enable me, through the gloom, to distinguish the people on them. The shrieks had gradually ceased; now and then the cry of some strong swimmer, who had hitherto bravely buffeted the sea, was heard ere he sank for the last time. Daylight was just breaking when, as I was standing up in the stern-sheets, I saw a person clinging to a piece of timber, and I determined, if possible, to save him. I pointed him out to the English seamen; and two of them, springing up, seized the oars from the hands of the Lascars, and by pulling away lustily we got up close to the spot. The man saw us coming. It was not without difficulty that we managed to haul him on board so as to avoid striking him or staving in the boat against the piece of wreck which had kept him up. To my surprise I found that he was the very gentleman who had assisted in forming the raft before the ship went down. I knew him by the case, which he still had secured to his side. He was so exhausted that for some minutes he could not speak, though he was evidently making an effort to do so. At length, beckoning me to put my ear down to his mouth, he asked in a low voice whether we had seen his wife and child, with the nurse. The only comfort I could afford him was by telling him that I had caught sight of several small rafts, and possibly they might be upon one of them. He had been washed away before he could secure himself when the ship foundered; and though he was carried down with her, on rising to the surface he had caught hold of the piece of wreck to which we had found him clinging.

"There we were, fourteen human beings in a small boat out in the middle of the Atlantic, the dark foaming seas surrounding us, without a particle of food or a drop of fresh water, while our two oars scarcely enabled us to keep her head to the sea, and save her from being capsized or swamped.

"I do not like to talk or even to think of the horrors which followed. Daylight had now come on, but all around was gloom, the dark clouds appearing like a pall just above our heads, and hanging round on either side, so as to circumscribe the horizon to the narrowest limits. Here and there I occasionally thought that I saw a few dark spots, which might have been the boats and rafts, or pieces of the wreck.

"The day passed by and there was no abatement of the gale. The Lascars had again taken the oars, but as night again approached, worn out with hunger and fatigue, they refused to pull any longer, and the gentleman offering to steer, the three other men and I took it by turns to labour at the oars.

"Thus the second night passed by. I had begun to feel faint and hungry, and to experience the pangs of thirst ; and, judging by my own sensations, I felt sure that, should we not fall in with a ship during the coming day, some of my companions would give way. Another morning dawned, but no sail was in sight. One of the Lascars lay dead in the bows, the rest were stretched out under the thwarts, unable even to continue baling, and apparently no longer caring what might become of them. The gentleman, though the most delicate-looking of us all, held out the best. His eye was constantly ranging over the ocean in search of the raft or boat which might contain those he loved best on earth. I had great difficulty in persuading him to let me take the helm again while he got a little sleep.

"As the day drew on the gale moderated, and the sea went down. So weak were the three other

Englishmen by this time, that I believe we should not otherwise have been able to prevent the boat being swamped. The Lascars were in a worse state. Two more died, and as their countrymen would not heave them overboard, we were obliged to do so. Eagerly we looked out for a sail, but none appeared. Before the next morning broke all the Lascars were dead, and I saw that one of my messmates was likely soon to follow them. Another, however, died before him, but ere the sun rose high in the heavens, he was gone.

"Besides the gentleman, only I and one man remained, the latter indeed was near his last gasp. I will not tell you what dreadful thoughts passed through my mind. Just then, as I was stooping down, I put my hand under the after seat. There, stowed away, was a large lump of grease. I felt round farther, and drew forth two bones with a considerable amount of meat on them. One of the dogs, I have no doubt, had made it his hiding place. The selfish thought came across me, that had the Lascars and the other two men been alive, this food would have gone very little way, but now it might support the existence of my two companions and me for another day or two. Eagerly I seized the putrid meat in my mouth, offering a piece to my companions. My messmate attempted to eat it, his jaws moved for a few seconds, then his head fell back. He had died in the effort. The gentleman could with difficulty swallow a few morsels. 'Water! water!' he muttered, 'without water it is too late.' I tried some of the grease, and felt revived.

"Not without difficulty we hove the last who had succumbed into the sea, and then the gentleman and I were alone. His spirits, which had hitherto kept up, were now, I saw, sinking. He beckoned

me to sit close to him, and I saw that he was
engaged in trying to loosen the strap which held
the case to his side. 'You are strong, my friend,'
he whispered, 'and may possibly survive till you
are picked up, I feel that I can trust you. Take
charge of this case—it contains an important docu-
ment, and jewels and money of considerable value.
Here, too, is a purse of gold, to that you are welcome,'
and he handed me a purse from his pocket. 'The
case I as a dying man commit to your charge, and
solemnly entreat you to take care of it for the benefit of my widow and orphan child, for the belief is
still strong within me that they survive. You will
find within this metal case full directions as to the
person to whom it is to be delivered.' He said this
with the greatest difficulty, and it seemed as if he
had exhausted all his strength in the effort. I promised to fulfil his wishes, and fully intended doing
so. He took my hand, and fixed his eyes on me, as
if he was endeavouring to read my thoughts. I
tried to make him take some more food, but he had
no strength to swallow it. Before the evening
closed in he too was gone.

" I had not the heart at once to throw him overboard. As I stood looking at him, prompted I
believe by the spirit of evil, an idea came into my
head. Should I reach shore the purse of gold
would enable me to enjoy myself for some time,
and perhaps I might obtain permanent employment
in a respectable position, instead of knocking about
at sea. I took off the dead man's clothes, and
dressed myself in them, though I was so weak that
the task was a difficult one. I then lifted the body
overboard. Having secured the box round my
waist, I placed the metal case and purse in my
pocket.

"I was alone, and though suffering greatly from thirst, I still felt that there was some life in me. I gazed around, but no sail was in sight. A light breeze only was blowing, and the sea had become tolerably calm, so eating a little more of the grease and meat, I lay down in the stern-sheets to sleep. I was awoke by feeling the water splashing over me. It was raining hard. There were two hats and a bucket in the boat. I quickly collected enough water to quench my thirst, and at once felt greatly revived. The rain continued long enough to enable me to fill the bucket. Had it not been for that shower I must have died.

"Two days longer I continued in the boat, when, just as the sun rose, my eyes fell on a sail in the horizon. How eagerly I watched her; she was standing towards me. Securing a shirt to the end of an oar, I waved it as high as I could reach. I was seen—the ship drew nearer. Being too weak to pull alongside I made no attempt to do so, and this being observed, the ship hove-to and lowered a boat, which soon had mine in tow. I was carefully lifted up the side, and on my dress being observed, I was at once treated as a gentleman. A cabin was given up to me, and every attention paid to my wants. I found that the ship was an emigrant vessel, outward bound, for Australia.

"I was some time in recovering my strength, and when I appeared among the passengers I took care to evade any questions put to me. I found the life on board very pleasant, and having purchased some clothes and other articles I was able to appear on an equality with the rest.

"We fell in with no other ship till Sydney was reached. I went on shore, purposing to amuse myself for a short time, and then return home and fulfil the dying request of my unfortunate companion in the boat. Would that I had gone on board a vessel sailing the very day of our arrival. Jack, never put off doing your duty, under the idea that it may be done a little time hence, lest that roaring lion we read of may catch hold of you and tempt you to put it off altogether. I remained on day after day, mixing in society, and rapidly spending my money. It was all gone, and then, Jack," and old Tom lowered his voice, " I did that vile deed—I broke open the box and took possession of the money I found within —the widow's and orphan's gold. I tried to persuade myself that they had certainly been lost. At first I only took the gold, intending to go home with the other articles; then I got to the notes. I had some difficulty in getting them changed, and was afraid of being discovered. At last I began to dispose of the jewels.

" At length I got a hint that I was suspected, and securing the case I once more dressed myself as a seaman, bought a chest, and got a berth on board a homeward-bound ship. I was miserable—conscience stung me—I could get no rest.

" The ship was cast away on the west coast of Ireland, and nearly all on board perished. I had secured about me the case, which still contained the parchment, the title-deeds of a large property, and a few jewels.

" I, with a few survivors, reached the shore. I was afraid to go back to England to deliver the case to the person to whom it was addressed, and so, making my way to Cork, where I found a ship bound for America, I went on board her.

" Jack, I have been knocking about ever since, my conscience never at rest, and yet not having the courage to face any danger I might incur, and make the only reparation in my power to those who, if still alive, I have deprived of their property. Now, notwithstanding what you say, there's something tells me that I have not long to live. I never had such a notion in my head before, but there it is now, and I cannot get rid of it. You are young and strong, and I want you to promise me, if you get home, to do what I ought to have done long ago. I will give you the case when we go below. Take it to the lawyer to whom it is addressed, and tell him all I have told you, and how it came into your possession, he'll believe you, I am sure, and though the money and most of the jewels are gone, the remainder will, I hope, be of value to the rightful owners."

I of course promised old Tom that I would do as he wished, at the same time I tried to persuade him to banish the forebodings which haunted him, from his mind. "That's more than I can do, Jack," he said, "I shouldn't mind the thoughts of death so much, if I could find the means of undoing all the ill I have done in the world—that's what tries me now." Unhappily neither I nor any one on board could tell the poor fellow that there is but one way by which sins can be washed away. I did indeed suggest that he should try and borrow a Bible from one of the gentlemen in the cabin, if they had one among them, for there was not one for'ard nor in the captain's or officers' berths.

When our watch was over, old Tom sat down on his chest, waiting till the rest of the watch had turned in and gone to sleep. He then cautiously opened his chest, and exhibited within, under his clothes, a small box, strongly bound with silver, and the metal case he had spoken of. "Here, Jack," he said, "I make you my heir, and give you the key of my chest : I'll tell the men to-morrow that I have done so, and let the captain and mates know it also, that there may be no dispute about the matter." I thanked old Tom, assuring him, at the same time, that I hoped not to benefit by his kindness.

In about three weeks we reached the mouth of the Columbia river. A strong gale from the westward had been blowing for several days, and as we came off the river a tremendous surf was seen breaking across the bar at its mouth. "I hope the captain won't attempt to take the vessel in," observed old Tom to me. "I have been in once while the sea was not so heavy by half as it is now, and our ship was nearly castaway." Still we stood on. Presently, however, the captain seemed to think better of it, and indifferent as he was to the lives of others, he apparently did not wish to lose his own, and the brig into the bargain. She was accordingly hauled to the wind, and we again stood off. It was only, however, to heave-to, when he ordered a boat to be lowered. He then directed the first mate to take four hands to go in her and sound the bar. The mate expostulated, and declared that the lives of all would be sacrificed in the attempt. "You are a coward, and are afraid," exclaimed the captain, stamping with rage. "Take old Tom and 'Happy Jack,' and two others," he called out their names. "No man shall justly say I am a coward," answered the mate ; "I'll go, but I'll take none but volunteers. My death and theirs will rest on your head, Captain Pyke." "I'll not go if the boy is sent," exclaimed old Tom; "but I am ready to go if another man takes his place." "Let me go, Tom," I said ; "if you and the mate go I am ready to accompany you." "No, Jack, I'll do no such thing," answered my friend. "You stay on board. Unless others step forward the boat won't go at all. The bar is not in a fit state for the vessel to cross, much less an open boat." The captain, however, seemed determined to go into the river, and now ordered another man to go instead of me. " I'll make you pay for this another day," he cried out, looking at me. I saw the mate shaking hands with several on board before he stepped into the boat. " Remember the case, Jack," said old Tom as he passed me, giving me a gripe by the hand. " You have got the key, lad."

The boat shoved off and pulled towards the bar. I watched her very anxiously; now she rose to the top of a roller, now she was hidden by the following one. Every instant I expected her to disappear altogether. I couldn't help thinking of what old Tom had said to me. Some time passed, when the captain ordered the helm to be put up, and the brig was headed towards the bar. He had been looking with his glass, and declared he had seen the mate's signal to stand in. The wind by this time had moderated. The brig was only under her topsails and mainsail, and I began to wonder at the mate's apprehensions. We had not stood on long when I saw the boat to the northward of us, much nearer the breakers than we were. She seemed to be carried by beyond the control of those in her. A strong current had caught hold of her. Presently she passed, not a pistol shot from us. The three men were shouting and shrieking for aid; old Tom was in the bows, sitting perfectly still; I could even distinguish the countenance of the mate, as he turned it with a reproachful glance, so it seemed to me, towards the captain. Beyond her appeared a high wall of hissing, foaming breakers, towards which she was driving. The captain seemed scarcely to notice the unfortunate men ; indeed his attention was occupied with attending to the brig, our position being extremely critical. I couldn't take my eyes off the boat. Would she be able even yet to stem the current and get back into smooth water ? Suddenly, however, it seemed as if the wall of foaming breakers came right down upon her, and she disappeared amidst them. A cry of horror escaped me. "We may be no better off ere long," I heard one of the men exclaim. He had scarcely spoken when the brig struck, and the foaming waters leaped up on either side, as if about to break on board. Another sea came roaring on, and she again moved forward. Again and again the brig struck, and at last seemed fixed.

Darkness was coming on, the foaming waters roared around us, frequently breaking on board, and we had to hold on to escape being washed away. The hatches had been battened down, or the vessel would have filled. She must have been a strong craft, or she could not have held together. The passengers behaved like brave men, though they evidently thought that it was the captain's obstinacy which had brought them into their present perilous position.

Hour after hour passed by, with no object discernible beyond the foaming waters surging round us. The men declared that they could hear the shrieks and cries of our shipmates. The captain swore at them as fools for saying so, declaring that their voices must long since have been silenced by the breakers. Every instant it seemed that the brig must go to pieces, and that we should be carried away to share their fate. Suddenly, however, I felt the brig move. The topsails were let fall and sheeted home, and we once more glided forward. In another hour we were safely at anchor in a sheltered bay within the mouth of the river.

The next morning several natives came off to us in their canoes. They were red-skinned painted savages, but appeared inclined to be friendly. By means of Mr. Duncan, who understood something of their language, they were told of the accident which had happened to the boat, and they undertook to search along the shore, in the possibility of any of the crew having escaped, and been washed on to the beach. On hearing of this my hopes of seeing old Tom again somewhat revived, though I scarcely believed it possible that any boat getting into those fearful breakers could have survived. Mr. Duncan and two of the other gentlemen agreed to accompany the savages.

In the evening the boat which had taken them on shore was seen coming off. I anxiously watched her. Besides those who had gone away, I distinguished one other person, he turned his face towards the vessel as the boat approached, and, to my delight, I saw that he was old Tom. "And so you have escaped, have you?" said the captain, as he stepped on board. "Yes, sir, but the others have gone where some others among us will be before long," answered Tom, gloomily, "and those who sent them there will have to render an account of their deeds." "What do you mean?" exclaimed the captain. "I leave that to others to answer," said Tom, walking forward.

He told me that the boat, on entering the surf, was immediately capsized, and that all hands were washed out of her. That he had managed to cling on with one man, and that when they got through the surf they had righted the boat, and picking up two of the oars, after bailing her out, had succeeded in paddling, aided by the current, some distance to the northward. On attempting to land the boat was again capsized. He had swam on shore, but the other poor fellow was drowned, and he himself was almost exhausted when met by the party who brought him back. "You see, Tom," I observed, " your prognostications have not come true, and you may still live to get back to old England again." " Oh no, Jack, though I have escaped this once, I am very sure my days are numbered," he answered ; do all I could, I was unable to drive this idea out of his head.

The crew were so indignant at the boat having been sent away, declaring that the captain wished to get rid of the mate and old Tom, that I felt sure another slight act of tyranny would produce a mutiny. While the gentlemen remained on board this was less likely to happen, but they were about to leave us, and take up their residence on shore.

Some time was occupied in landing their goods and stores, and then we found that we were to proceed to the northward, on a trading voyage with the Indians, and that Mr. Duncan was to accompany us. We had also received on board an Indian, who had long resided with the whites, and who was to act as our interpreter.

A fair wind carried us over the bar, and, steering to the northward, we continued on for several days, till we brought up in a deep bay, on the shore of which was situated a large native village. Large numbers of the Indians came off in their canoes, with furs to exchange for cutlery, cotton goods, looking-glasses, beads, and other ornaments. Many of them were fine looking, independent fellows, but veritable savages, dressed in skins, their heads adorned, after their fashion, with feathers, shells, and the teeth of different animals. The captain treated them with great contempt, shouting at them, and ordering them here and there, as if they were beings infinitely inferior to himself. I saw them frequently turn angry glances at him, but they did not otherwise exhibit any annoyance. One day, however, he had a dispute with one of their chiefs about a matter of barter, when, losing his temper, he struck the savage and knocked him over on the deck. The Indian, recovering himself, cast a fierce glance at him, then, folding his arms, walked away, uttering some words to his companions, which we did not understand.

The next day, Mr. Duncan, who had gone on shore, returned on board hurriedly, with the interpreter, and warned the captain that the Indians intended to take vengeance for the insult their chief had received. The captain laughed, declaring that he did not fear what ten times the number of savages who as yet had come on board, would venture to do. "They are daring fellows, though, Captain Pyke, and treacherous, and cunning in the extreme," observed Mr. Duncan. "Take my advice and keep them out of the ship. We have already done a fair trade here, and the natives have not many more skins to dispose of." "I am not to be frightened as other people are," answered the captain, scornfully. "If they have no skins they will not bring them, and if they have, I am not the man to be forgetful of the interests of the Company, by refusing to trade."

This was said on deck in the hearing of the crew. "I'll tell you what, Jack," observed old Tom to me, "the captain will repent not following Mr. Duncan's advice. If the Indians come on board, keep by me —we shall have to fight for our lives. I know these people. When they appear most friendly, they are often meditating mischief."

That very evening several canoes came off, and in them was the chief whom the captain had knocked down. He seemed perfectly friendly, smiling and shaking hands with the captain as if he had entirely forgotten the insult he had received.

When the savages took their departure, they were apparently on the best of terms with us all.

CHAPTER VI.

THE next morning we were preparing to put to sea, when two large canoes came off, each carrying about twenty men. As they exhibited a considerable number of furs, the captain allowed them to come on board, and trade commenced as usual. In the meantime, three other canoes came off with a similar number of men, and a larger quantity of furs of the most valuable descriptions. They also were allowed to come up the side like the rest.

"Jack, I don't like the look of things," said old Tom.

"Do you observe that the savages are wearing cloaks such as they have not appeared in before. Just come down for'ard with me."

I followed Tom below. "Here," he said, "fasten this case under your jacket. If the savages attack us, we will jump into the boat astern ; they will be too much intent on plunder to follow us, and we will make our escape out to sea. I propose to do this for your sake. As for me, I would as lief remain and fight it out. I have mentioned my sus-

picions to several of the men, and advised them to
have an eye on the handspikes ; with them we may
keep the savages at bay till we can make good our
retreat."

I asked him why he did not warn the captain.
" Because he is mad, and would only laugh at me,"
he answered. " Mr. Duncan and the interpreter
have already done so, and they are as well aware as
I am that mischief is brewing."

On going on deck, we saw the captain speaking to
the Indians, and ordering them to return to their
canoes. They appeared as if they were going to
obey him, when suddenly, each man drawing a
weapon from beneath his cloak uttered a fearful
yell, and leaped at the officers and us. The captain,
with only a jack-knife in his hand, defended himself
bravely, killing four of his savage assailants.

Led by old Tom, I, with three or four other men,
fought our way aft to join the officers, intending,
should we be overpowered, to leap, as we had proposed, into the boat. I saw poor Mr. Duncan
struck down and hove into a canoe alongside. The
captain was apparently trying to reach the cabin,
probably to get his fire-arms, when he fell, struck by
a hatchet on the head.

" Follow me," cried Tom. " We may reach the
boat through the cabin windows." As he said this,
he sprang down the companion-hatch, I and two
others following him. The remainder of our number were overtaken by the savages before they could
reach it. The last, Andrew Pearson, our boatswain,
contrived to secure the hatch. This gave us time to
get hold of the fire-arms fastened against the bulkheads, and to load and place them ready for use on
the table. There were at least a dozen muskets,
and as many brace of pistols. Had these been in

our hands on deck, we should probably have driven the savages overboard, or they would have been deterred from making the attack. With them, we might now defend our lives against vastly superior numbers.

The scuffle on deck was still going on, the yells of the savages rising above the stifled groans and cries of our unfortunate shipmates. They soon ceased, and then arose a shout of triumph from our enemies, and we knew that we were the only survivors. But we too were in a desperate plight. Tom was severely wounded, and the boatswain and the other man had received several gashes. I, indeed, thanks to the way in which Tom had defended me, was the only person unhurt.

"Green, do you look after the hatchway," said Pearson to the other man who had escaped. "Tom, do you and Jack show your muskets through the stern windows, I have some work to do. The savages think they have us in a trap, but they are mistaken." He opened, as he spoke, a hatch which led to the magazine, and I saw him uncoiling a long line of match, one end of which he placed in the magazine, while he led the other along the cabin to the stern-port. Meantime, the savages had all clambered on board, and were shrieking and shouting in the most fearful manner, crowding down into the hold, as we could judge by the sounds which reached us, and handing up the rich treasures they found there.

"No time to be lost," said Pearson, hauling up the boat. He went to the locker, and collected all the provisions he could find. "Jump in, Tom and Jack," he said. "Now for the fire-arms." He handed them in, and told us to place them along the thwarts, ready for use. "Now, Green," he said in a low voice, "jump in." We three were now in the boat, which was hidden under the counter from those on deck. He struck a light, and placed it to the slow match, and, having ascertained that it was burning, slipped after us into the boat, in which the mast was fortunately stepped.

"Jack, do you take the helm, and steer directly for the mouth of the harbour," he said, cutting the painter and seizing an oar. Tom and Green did the same, and pulled away lustily. We had already got several fathoms from the vessel before we were perceived. The sail had been placed ready for hoisting. It was run up and sheeted home. The savages were about to jump into one of the canoes, and chase us, but three muskets pointed towards them made them hesitate. We were rapidly slipping away from the doomed brig. We could see the savages dancing and leaping on deck, their shouts and yells coming over the water towards us.

"They will dance to another tune soon," muttered Pearson between his teeth.

He and the other two had again taken to the oars. Even now a flight of arrows might have reached us, but fortunately the savages had not brought their bows with them, and probably that was the chief reason why they had not ventured to pursue us. They well knew that several of their number would have been shot down with our bullets had they made the attempt. Still we could see some of the chiefs apparently trying to persuade their warriors to follow us, and we knew that though we might fight till all our ammunition was expended, we should at last be overwhelmed by numbers.

Our chance of ultimate escape seemed small indeed. "They will not come," said Pearson. "See!" We had got half-a-mile or more from the brig, when a deep thundering sound reached our ears. It seemed as if the whole vessel was lifted out of the water, while up into the air shot her main-mast and spars, and fragments of her deck and bul-warks, and other pieces of timber, mingled with countless human bodies, with limbs torn off and mangled in a fearful manner. At the same time the canoes with those who had escaped were paddling with frantic energy towards the shore, probably be-lieving that the Great Spirit had sent forth one of his emissaries to punish them for their treachery to the white people. We concluded that some such idea as this was entertained by them, as we saw no canoes coming off in pursuit of us.

Rowing and sailing, we continued to make our way out to the open ocean. It was blowing fresh but, the wind coming off shore, the sea was tolerably calm, and we agreed that at all events it was better to undergo the dangers of a long voyage in an open boat than trust ourselves in the power of the revengeful savages. We had reached the mouth of the harbour, and could still see the village far off on its shore, when, to our dismay, we found the sea breeze setting in. We had accordingly to haul our wind, though we still hoped to weather the headland which formed its southern point, and get an offing.

Tom all this time had uttered no complaint, though I saw the blood flowing down his side. The boatswain and Green had, with my help, bound up their wounds. I wanted Tom to let me assist him. "No," he said; "it's of no use. If you were to swathe me up, I could not pull. It will be time enough for that when we get round the headland." He was evidently getting weaker, and at last the boatswain persuaded him to lay in his oar, and try to stop the blood. The wounds were in his back and neck, inflicted by the savages as he fought his way onward to the cabin. I bound our handkerchiefs round him as well as I could; but it was evident that he was not fit for rowing, and that the only chance of the blood stopping was for him to remain perfectly quiet.

During the last tack we made I fancied, as I looked up the harbour, that I saw the canoes coming out. I told the boatswain. "We will give them a warm reception, if they come near us," he answered.

I felt greatly relieved when we at last weathered the point, and were now able to stand along shore, though we couldn't get the offing which was desirable.

Night was coming on. The weather looked threatening, and our prospects of ultimately escaping were small.

At last we got so near the surf that the boatswain determined to put the boat about and stand out to sea. Although the other tack might bring us almost in front of the harbour's mouth, it was the safest course to avoid being cast on shore.

The night came on very dark, but the wind was moderate, and there was not much sea. Still the weather was excessively cold, and my companions suffered greatly from their wounds. Tom had been placed in the stern-sheets near me. Though he said less, he suffered more than the rest, and I could every now and then hear low groans escaping from his bosom. At last I heard him calling me. "Jack," he whispered, "what I told you is coming true. I am going; I feel death creeping over me. Remember the case. Do all you know I ought to have done. I have been a great sinner; but you once said there is a way by which all sins can be blotted out. I believe in that way. **Jack,** give me your hand. It's darker than ever; and I am cold, very cold." He pressed my hand, and I heard him murmuring to himself. It might have been a prayer, but his words were indistinct; I could not understand what he said. I kept steering with one hand, looking up at the sails, and casting a glance now and then at him, while the other two men pulled away to keep the boat to windward. Presently I felt his fingers relax; an icy chill came from his hand. I knew too well that my friend was dead. It was some time before I could bring myself to tell the boatswain what had happened. " Poor fellow ! But it may be the lot of all of us before another day is over," he said; " yet, as men, we will struggle to the last."

The night passed on, and we still persevered in endeavouring to obtain an offing, though so indistinct was the land that we could not tell whereabouts we were. What was our dismay, when morning broke, to find that we were directly off the mouth of the harbour, and at such a distance that the keen eyes of the savages on the hills around might easily perceive our sail. We at once put the boat about, hoping to get again to the south'ard before we were discovered. " It's too late," cried Green; " I see the canoes coming." " We must fight them, then," said the daring boatswain, calmly. " We don't just expect mercy at their hands after the treat we gave them," and he laughed at the fearful act he had committed. Still I thought what could we three, in a small boat, with our dozen muskets, do against a whole fleet of fierce savages.

We could now see the canoes coming out of the harbour. The sea was smooth, and they would without fail venture after us. Our only chance of escape seemed in a sudden gale springing up, but of that there was little probability. I was turning my eyes anxiously towards the offing in hopes of seeing signs of a stronger breeze coming, when I caught sight of a sail. I pointed her out to the boatswain. "She is a large vessel," he exclaimed, "and standing this way." "Perhaps the savages will be more than ever anxious to catch us, for fear we should persuade the people on board yonder ship to punish them for what they have done," I observed. "They will catch us if they can," answered Pearson; "but they will have to pay a good price yet if they make the attempt," and he cast his eyes at the muskets which lay ready loaded. The canoes were drawing nearer and nearer, and we could now distinguish the figures of the plumed warriors as they stood up in the bows. The boat at the same time was slipping pretty quickly through the water. "The breeze is freshening," I observed; "we may escape them yet." "I don't much care if we do or do not," said Pearson; "I should like to knock over a few of these boasting fellows; we may hit them long before they can get near enough to hurt us." I for my part did not wish to see more of the savages killed, for they had only followed the instinct of their untutored natures, and we had already inflicted a terrible punishment on them in return. In a few minutes the breeze came down even stronger than before, and greatly to my satisfaction, the canoes appeared to be scarcely gaining on us, even if they did so at all. I continued to give a glance every now and then at the ship, for I was afraid after all she might alter her course, and stand away from us.

At length, to my joy, I saw the savages in the canoes cease paddling. They apparently were afraid of venturing farther out into the ocean, or saw that it would be hopeless to attempt overtaking us. For

some minutes they waited, as if holding a consulta-
tion, and then round they paddled and made their
way back into the harbour.

"Just like them," exclaimed Pearson. "Those
cowardly red-skins will never fight unless they can
take their enemies at an advantage."

We had to make several tacks towards the ship,
and then when we got near enough for the sound of
our muskets to reach her, we fired several as a signal.
They were at length, we concluded, heard on board.
She kept away towards us. She drew nearer. We
saw that she was a whaler, with the English colours
flying at the peak. She rounded to, and we went
alongside. "What has happened?" exclaimed several
voices, as old Tom's body was seen lying in the stern-
sheets. A few words told our tale. I was able to
climb up the side, but Pearson and Green were so
stiff from their wounds that they had to be helped
up. They were far more hurt indeed than they had
supposed, especially Pearson; but his dauntless spirit
had hitherto kept him up. Our boat was hoisted
on board, and old Tom's body was taken out and
laid on deck. We were treated with great kindness,
and the captain, greatly to my satisfaction, volunteered to give old Tom Christian burial. He had, as
we supposed, intended to go into the harbour to
obtain wood and water, and to trade with the
natives; but when he heard of what had occurred he
resolved to steer for a port farther south, and he
told me that he was very grateful to us for giving
him warning of the danger which he otherwise would
have run.

In the evening I saw my poor friend lashed up in
a hammock, and committed to his ocean grave.

All night long I was dreaming of him and of the
dreadful scenes I had witnessed,

The ship was the *Juno*. Her commander, Captain Knox, was a very different sort of person to my late captain; and from his kind manner, and the way he spoke to the officers and men, he seemed truly to act the part of a father to his crew. The ship had been out a year and a half, and it was expected she would remain another year in the Pacific.

Though I was anxious to get home, yet when the captain asked me to enter on board, I was very glad to do so. Pearson continued to suffer fearfully from his wounds. Whether the deed he had done preyed on his mind, I cannot say; but a high fever coming on, he used to rave about the savages, and the way he had blown them up. At the moment he committed the deed I daresay he had persuaded himself that he was only performing a justifiable act of vengeance. The day before we entered the harbour to which we were bound he died, and poor Green did not long survive him, so that I alone was left of all the crew of the ill-fated *Fox*.

CHAPTER VII.

THE captain of the *Juno* took every precaution to prevent her being surprised by the Indians. Boarding nettings were triced up round the ship every night, and the watch on deck had arms ready at hand. None of the natives were allowed to come on board, and only two or three canoes were permitted alongside at a time. We judged by their manner, though they were willing enough to trade, that they had already heard of what had occurred to the northward.

Having got our wood and water on board, we

again put to sea, cruising in various parts of the ocean known to be frequented by whales. A bright look-out was kept for their spouts as the monsters rose to the surface to breathe. The instant a spout was seen all was life and animation on board; the boats were lowered, generally two or three at a time, and away they pulled to be ready to attack the whale as it again rose to the surface. I remember, the first time I saw one of the monsters struck, I shouted and jumped about the deck as eagerly as if I myself were engaged in the work. Now I saw the lines flying out of the boat at a rapid rate, as the animal sounded; now the men in the boats hauled it in again, as the whale rose once more to the surface; now they pulled on, and two more deadly harpoons were plunged into its sides, with several spears; now they backed to avoid the lashing strokes of its powerful tail; now the creature was seen to be in its death-flurry, tumbling about and turning over and over in its agony. At length it lay an inert mass on the surface, and the boats came back, towing it in triumph. Next there was the work of "cutting in," or taking off the blubber which surrounded it; the huge body being turned round and round during the operation, as the men stood on it cutting off with their sharp spades huge strips, which were hoisted with tackles on deck. Last of all came the "trying out," when the blubber, cut into pieces, was thrown into huge caldrons on deck, with a fire beneath them; the crisp pieces, from which the oil had been extracted, serving as fuel. It was a curious scene when night came on, and fires blazed up along the deck, surrounded by the crew, begrimed with oil and smoke, looking like beings of another world engaged in some fearful incantation.

This scene was repeated over and over again. We visited several islands in the Pacific. At some, where Christian missionaries had been at work, the inhabitants showed by their conduct that they were worthy of confidence; but at others the captain deemed it necessary to be constantly on his guard, lest they might attempt to cut off the crew and take possession of the ship, as we heard had frequently occurred.

At length, to my delight and that of all the crew, the last cask we had on board was filled with oil, and with a deeply-laden ship we commenced our homeward voyage. We encountered a heavy gale going round the Horn, but the old *Juno* weathered it bravely, though, as she strained a good deal, we had afterwards to keep the pumps going for an hour or so during each watch. We, however, made our way at a fair rate northward, and once more crossed the line.

It may seem surprising that I had not hitherto examined the metal case which old Tom had committed to my charge. The box itself I had resolved not to open. I did not suppose that I should be induced to act as he had done, but yet I thought it wiser not to run the risk of temptation. We for several days lay becalmed, and one evening, while the crew were lying about the decks overcome with the heat, I stowed myself away for'ard, at a distance from the rest, and drew the paper out of the case. Great was my surprise to find that it was addressed to my own father It contained a reference to the parchment in the box, and gave a list both of the jewels, the notes, and gold. The writer spoke of his wife and infant son, and charged my father, should any accident happen to him, to act as their guardian and friend as well as their legal adviser. The letter was signed "Clement Leslie."

"This is strange," I thought. "Then there can

be no doubt that little Clem is the very child old Tom saw placed in his nurse's arms on the raft, and his poor mother must have been washed away when the ship went down. Those Indian nurses, I have often heard, will sacrifice their own lives for the sake of preserving the children committed to their charge, and Clem's nurse must have held him fast in her arms, in spite of the buffeting of the waves and the tossing of the raft during that dreadful night when the Indiaman went down ; and if she had any food, I dare say she gave it to him rather than eat it herself. But, poor fellow, what may have happened to him since we parted."

I now felt more anxious than ever to reach home, and longed for the breeze to spring up which might carry us forward through the calm latitudes. It came at last, and the *Juno* again made rapid progress homeward. We were bound up the Irish Channel to Liverpool; when, however, we got within about a week's sail of the chops of the Channel, it came on to blow very hard. The leaks increased, and we were now compelled to keep the pumps going during nearly the whole of each watch. The weather was very thick, too, and no observations could be taken. The crew were almost worn out; yet there was no time for rest. The gale was blowing from the south-west, and the sea running very high, when in the middle watch the look-out shouted the startling cry of "Land! on the starboard bow." The yards were at once braced sharply up, and soon afterwards the captain ordered the ship to be put about. We were carrying almost more canvas than she could bear, but yet it would not then do to shorten sail. Just as the ship was in stays, a tremendous squall struck her, and in an instant the three masts went by the board.

There we lay on a lee shore, without a possibility of getting off it. The order was at once given to range the cables, that immediately the water was sufficiently shallow to allow of it we might anchor.

I will not describe that dreadful night. Onward the ship drove towards the unknown shore. We had too much reason to dread that it was the western coast of Ireland, fringed by reefs and rugged rocks. As we drove on it grew more and more fearfully distinct. We fired guns of distress, in the faint hope that assistance might be sent to us; but no answering signal came. Too soon the roar of the surf reached our ears, and it became fearfully probable that the ship and her rich cargo, with all on board, would become the prey of the waves. I secured the precious box and case as usual, determined, if I could save my own life, to preserve them. The lead was continually hove, and at last the captain ordered the anchors to be let go. They held the ship but for a few minutes; then a tremendous sea struck her, and sweeping over her deck, they parted, and again onward she drove. A few minutes more only elapsed before she struck the rocks, and the crashing and rending sounds of her timbers warned us that before long she would be dashed into a thousand fragments. The sea was breaking furiously over the wreck, and now one, now another of the crew was washed away. I was clinging with others to a part of the bulwarks, when I felt them loosening beneath us. Another sea came, and we were borne forward towards the shore. For an instant I was beneath the boiling surf; when I rose again my companions were gone, and in a few seconds I found myself dashed against a rock. I clung to it for my life, then scrambled on, my only thought being to get away from the raging waters. I succeeded at length in scrambling out of their reach, and lay down on a dry ledge to rest. I must have dropped to sleep or fainted from fatigue. When I came to myself, the sun was up, and I heard voices below me. The tide had fallen, and numbers of country people were scrambling along the rocks, and picking up whatever was thrown on shore. I managed to get on my feet and wave to them. Several came up to me, and the tones of their voices showed me at once that they were Irish.

Out of the whole crew, I was the only person who had been saved, and I was very doubtful how I might be treated. However, I wronged them. It was a matter of dispute among several who should take charge of me; and at length a young woman, whose cottage was not far off, carried me up to it. She and her husband gave me the best of everything they had; that is to say, as many potatoes and as much buttermilk and bacon as I could swallow. I was so eager to get home that, after a night's rest, I told them I wished to start on my journey. I was, I knew, on the west of Ireland, and I hoped that, if I could manage to get to Cork, I might from thence find means of crossing to England. Though my host had no money to give me, he agreed to drive me twenty miles on the way, promising to find a friend who would pass me on; and his wife pressed on me a change of linen, and a few other articles in a bundle. With these I started on my long journey.

I was not disappointed, for when I told my story I was fully believed, and I often got help where I least expected it.

At length I reached Cork, where I found a vessel just sailing for Liverpool. The captain agreed to give me a free passage, and at last I safely landed on the shores of old England. I must confess that I had more difficulty after this in making my way homeward, and by the time I reached the neighbourhood of my father's house my outer clothing, at all events, was pretty well worn to rags and tatters.

CHAPTER VIII.

IT was the early summer when one evening I came in sight of my home. The windows and doors were open. Without hesitation I walked up the steps, forgetting the effect which my sudden appearance might produce on my family. One of my youngest sisters was in the passage. I beckoned to her. "What do you want?" she asked; "you must not stop here; go away." "What! don't you know me?" I asked. "No," she answered; "who are you?" "Jack—your brother Jack," I answered. On this she ran off into the drawing-room, and I heard her exclaim, "There's a great big beggar boy, and he says he is Jack—our brother Jack." "Oh no, that cannot be!" I heard one of my other sisters reply. "Poor Jack was drowned long ago in the *Naiad.*" "No, he was not," I couldn't help exclaiming; and without more ado I ran forward. My appearance created no small commotion among three or four young ladies who were seated in the room. "Go away; how dare you venture in here?" exclaimed one or two of them. "Will you not believe me?" I cried. "I am Jack, I assure you, and I hope soon to convince you of the fact." "It is Jack, I know it is!" exclaimed one of them, jumping up and coming forward. I knew her in an

instant to be Grace Goldie, though grown almost
into a young woman. "It is Jack, I am sure it
is," she added, taking my hand and leading me
forward. "Oh, how strange that you do not know
him!" My sisters now came about me, examining
me with surprised looks. "How strange, Grace,"
said one; "surely you must be mistaken?" "No,
I am sure I am not," answered Grace, looking into
my face, and putting back the hair from my fore-
head; "Are you not Jack?" "Yes, I believe I
am," I answered, "though if you did not say so I
should begin to doubt the fact, since Ann, and
Mary, and Jane, do not seem to know me." "Well,
I do believe it is Jack," cried Jane, coming up and
taking my other hand, though I was so dirty that
she did not, I fancy, like to kiss me. "So he is—
he must be!" cried the others; and now, in spite of
my tattered dress, their sisterly affection got the
better of all other considerations, and they threw
their arms about me like kind girls as they really
were, and I returned their salutes, in which Grace
Goldie came in for a share, with long unaccustomed
tears in my eyes. Just then a shriek of astonishment was heard, and there stood Aunt Martha at
the door. "Who have you got there?" she exclaimed. "It's Jack come back," answered my
sisters and Grace in chorus. "Jack come back!
impossible!" cried out Aunt Martha, in what I
thought sounded a tone of dismay. "Yes, I am
Jack, I assure you," I said, going up to her; "and I
hope to be your very dutiful and affectionate nephew,
whatever you may once have thought me;" and I
took her hand and raised it to my lips. "If you
are Jack I am glad to see you," she said, her feelings
softening; "and it will at all events be a comfort
to your poor mother to know that you are not

drowned." " My mother! where is she ?" I asked
—" I trust she is not ill." "Yes, she is, I am sorry
to say, and up-stairs in bed," replied my aunt; " but
I'll go and break the news to her, lest the sound of
all this hubbub should reach her ears, and make her
inquire what is the matter."

I had now time to ask about the rest of my family.
My father was out, but was soon expected home,
and in the meantime, while Aunt Martha had gone
to tell my mother, by my sisters' advice I went into
the bedroom of one of my brothers, and washed, and
dressed myself in his clothes. By the time Aunt
Martha came to look for me I was in a more pre-
sentable condition than when I entered the house.

I need not dwell on my interview with my mother.
She had no doubts about my identity, but drawing
me to her, kissed me again and again, as most
mothers would do, I suspect, under similar circumstances. She was unwilling to let me go, but at
length Aunt Martha, suggesting that I might be
hungry, a fact that I could not deny, as I was almost
ravenous, I quickly joined the merry party round
the tea-table, when I astonished them not a little by
the number of slices of ham and bread which I
shortly devoured. My father soon arrived. He was
not much given to sentiment, but he wrung my hand
warmly, and his mind was evidently greatly relieved
on finding that his plan for breaking me of my
desire for a sea life had not ended by consigning me
to a watery grave. He was considerably astonished,
and evidently highly pleased, when I put into his
hands the box and case which old Tom had given
into my care ; and I told him how I had fallen in, on
board the *Naiad*, with the boy I fully believed to
be Mr. Clement Leslie's heir.

"This is indeed strange," he muttered, " very

strange, and we must do our best to find him out,
Jack. It's a handsome estate, and it will be a pity
if the young fellow is not alive to enjoy it. I must
set Simon Munch to work at once." "Perhaps if
the Russian frigate has returned home, we may learn
from her officers what has become of him," I sug-
gested. "We will think the matter over. Would
you like a trip to Russia, Jack?" "Above all
things, sir," I answered. "I could start to-morrow
if it were necessary ;" though I confess I felt very
unwilling to run away again so soon from home,
especially as my mother was so ill. Perhaps, also,
Grace Goldie entered somewhat into my considerations.

Next morning while we were at breakfast, and
my father was looking over the newspaper, he exclaimed, " We are in luck, Jack ! Did you not say
that the name of the Russian frigate which picked
you up was the *Alexander?* I see that she has
just arrived at Spithead, from China and the Western
Pacific. If so, there is not a moment to be lost, for
she will probably be off again in a few days. You
must start at once. Get your sisters to pack up
such of your brother's things as will fit you, and I'll
order a post-chaise to the door immediately." " I
shall be ready, sir, directly I have swallowed another
egg or two, and a few more slices of toast," I
answered. " Munch must go with you, that there
may be no mistake about the matter," said my father.
" He will be of great assistance."

All seemed like a dream. In a quarter of an
hour I was rattling away as fast as a couple of
posters could go, along the road to London. I sat
in a dignified and luxurious manner, feeling myself
a person of no little consequence—remembering
that, at the same hour on the previous day, I had

been trudging along the road ragged and hungry, with some doubt as to the reception I was to meet with at home. My tongue was kept going all the time, for Munch wished to hear all about my adventures. " Well, Master Jack, I am glad to have you back," he said. " To tell the truth, my conscience was a little uncomfortable at the part I had taken in shipping you off on board the collier, though I might have known—" he cast a quizzical look at me—" that those are never drowned who are——"

" Born to end their lives comfortably in bed," I added, interrupting him. " You needn't finish the sentence in the way you were about to do ; I was never much of a favourite of yours, Mr. Munch, I know."

" I hope we shall be better friends in future, Master Jack," he remarked. " You used, you know, to try my temper not a little sometimes."

As the old clerk was accustomed to long and sudden journeys, we stopped nowhere, except for a few minutes to get refreshments, till we rattled up to the George Inn at Portsmouth.

Much to our satisfaction, we heard from the waiter that the Russian frigate was still at Spithead, and as the weather was fine, we hurried down the High Street, intending at once to engage a wherry and go off to her. As we reached the point a man-of-war's boat pulled up, and several officers stepped on shore. " That is not the English uniform," observed Munch ; " perhaps they have come from the Russian frigate." He was right, I was sure, for I thought that I recognised the countenances of several I had known on board the *Alexander.* Among them was a tall, slight young man, dressed as a sub-lieutenant. I looked at him earnestly, scanning his features. It might be Clement, yet I should not under other circumstances have thought it possible. The young man stopped, observing the way I was regarding him, and I began to doubt that he could be Clement, as he did not appear to know me. I could bear the uncertainty no longer, so, walking up to him, I said, "I am Happy Jack! Don't you know me?" His whole countenance lighted up. With a cry of pleasure he seized both my hands, gazing earnestly in my face. "Jack, my dear fellow, Jack!" he exclaimed. "You alive, and here! Happy you may be, but not so happy as I am to see you. I mourned you as lost, for I could not hope that you had escaped a second time." His surprise was great indeed when I told him I came especially to search for him, and we at once agreed to repair to the "George," that I might give him the important information I had to afford, and settle, with the aid of Mr. Munch, what course it would be advisable for him to pursue.

He was overwhelmed, as may be supposed, with astonishment and thankfulness when I told him of the wonderful way in which I had become possessed of the title-deeds and jewels, which would, I hoped, establish his claims to a fair estate.

This matter occupied some time. "With regard to quitting the ship," he observed, "there will, I trust, be no difficulty. I am but a supernumerary on board, and as I could not regularly enter the service till the frigate returned to Russia, the captain will be able to give me my discharge when I explain the circumstances in which I am placed."

Having settled our plans, Mr. Munch and I went on board with Clement. The captain at once agreed to what Clement wished, though he expressed his regret at losing him. My friend the doctor recog-

nised me, and treated me, as did several of the other
officers, with much kindness and politeness. I was,
however, too anxious to get Clement home to accept
their courtesy, and the next morning we were again
on the road northward.

Clement had studied hard while on board the
Russian frigate, and had become a polished and
gentlemanly young man, in every way qualified for
the position he was destined to hold. He was made
not a little of by my family, and though at one time
I felt a touch of jealousy at the preference I fancied
he showed to Grace Goldie, he soon relieved my
fears by telling me that he hoped to become the
husband of one of my sisters.

My father, after a considerable amount of labour,
proved his identity with the son of Mr. Clement
Leslie, who perished with his wife at sea, and
established his claims to the property.

I had had quite enough of a "life on the ocean
wave," and though I had no great fancy for working
all day at a desk, I agreed to enter my father's
office and tackle to in earnest, my incentive to
labour, I confess, being the hope of one day becoming the husband of Grace Goldie. We married,
and I have every reason still to call myself "**Happy
Jack.**"

THE
"San Fiorenzo" and her Captain.

NARRATED BY ADMIRAL M———.

———◦◦———

HERE was not a happier ship in the service, when I joined her towards the end of the year 1794, than the gallant *San Fiorenzo*, Captain Sir Harry Burrard Neale, and those were not days when ships were reckoned little paradises afloat, even by enthusiastic misses or sanguine young midshipmen. They were generally quite the other thing.

The crews of many ships found it that other thing, and the officers, of course, found it so likewise. If the men are not contented, the officers must be uncomfortable; and, at the same time, I will say, from my experience, that when a ship gained the title of a hell-afloat, it was always in consequence of the officers not knowing their duty, or not doing it. Pride, arrogance, and an utter disregard for the feelings of those beneath them in rank, was too prevalent among the officers of the service, and was the secret of the calamitous events which occasionally happened about that time.

My noble commander was not such an one as

87

those of whom I have spoken. There were some like him, but not many his equals. I may truly say of him "that he belonged to the race of admirals of which the navy of Old England has a right to be proud ; that he was a perfect seaman, and a perfect gentleman." "He was one of the most humane, brave, and zealous commanders that ever trod a deck, to whom every man under him looked up as a father." I was with him for many, very many years—from my boyish days to manhood,—and I may safely say that I never saw him in a passion, or even out of temper, though I have seen him indignant ; and never more so than when merit— the merit of the junior officers of the service—has been overlooked or disregarded. I never heard him utter an oath, and I believe firmly that he never allowed one to escape his lips. I will say of him what I dare say of few men, that, in the whole course of his life, he was never guilty of an act unworthy of the character of a Christian and a gentleman. I was with him when his career was run—when, living in private on his own estate, the brave old sailor, who had ever kept himself unspotted from the world, spent his days in "visiting the fatherless and widows in their affliction"—walking from cottage to cottage, with his basket of provisions or medicines, or books, where the first were not required.

Genuine were the tears shed on his grave, and hearty was the response as the following band gave forth the air of "The Fine Old English Gentleman, all of the Olden Time !"

And now, on the borders of his estate, visible afar over the Solent Sea,* there stands a monument, raised

* The "Solent Sea" is the name of the channel between the Isle of Wight and the mainland.

by his sovereign and by those who knew and loved him well, all eager to add their testimony to his worth. But yet he lives in the heart of many a seaman, and will live while one remains who served under his command. But, avast! whither am I driving? My feelings have carried me away.

After what I have said, it is not surprising that the *San Fiorenzo* should have been a happy ship. Her captain made her so. From the highest to the lowest, all trusted him; all knew that he had their interest at heart—all loved him. The *San Fiorenzo* might have been a happy ship under an inferior commander—that is possible; but I doubt very much whether her crew would have done what they did do under any officer not possessed of those high qualities for which Sir Harry was so eminently distinguished. The *San Fiorenzo* was highly honoured, for she was the favourite ship, or rather, Sir Harry was the favourite captain of His Majesty George the Third, who, let people say what they will of him, was truly the sailors' friend, and wished to be his subjects' friend, as far as he had the power. Sir Harry was a favourite, not because he was a flatterer, but because the King knew him to be an honest man.

George the Third, as is well known, was very fond of spending the summer months at Weymouth, whence he could easily put to sea in his yacht, or on board a man-of-war, placed at his disposal. He seemed never to tire of sailing, especially with Sir Harry.

Whist was the constant game in the royal cabins. Sir Harry, who did everything as well as he could, though far from a good player, often beat the King, who was an indifferent one. Lord A——, a practised courtier, was, on the contrary, a remarkably good one, and generally beat Sir Harry. When, however, Lord A—— played with the King, His Majesty always came off victorious. The King used to pretend to be exceedingly puzzled.

" It's very odd—very odd. I beat Lord A——, Lord A—— beats Sir Harry, and Sir Harry beats me. How can it be—how can it be ?"

The King was always anxious to stand out to sea, so as to lose sight of land. This, however, was too dangerous an amusement to allow him. Sir Harry's plan was to put the ship's head off-shore, and to make all sail. This satisfied the King, who was then easily persuaded to go below to luncheon, dinner, or tea, or to indulge in his favourite game. Sail was soon again quietly shortened, and the ship headed in for the shore. Sometimes the King seemed rather surprised that we should have made the land again so soon ; but whether or not he suspected a trick, I cannot say. His only remark was, " All right, Sir Harry ; you are always right."

It was impossible for a monarch to be more condescending and affable than was the good old King to all on board. He used to go among the men, and talk to them in the most familiar way, inquiring about their adventures and family histories, and evidently showing a sympathy with their feelings and ideas. Did they love the old King? Ay, there was not a man of them who would not gladly have died for him. It was the same with the midshipmen and officers. He used to delight in calling up us youngsters, and would chat with us as familiarly as would any private gentleman. He showed his real disposition, when able thus to cast aside the cares of state, and to give way to the kindly feelings of his heart. I say again, in that respect the King and his captain were worthy of each other. The following anecdote will prove it :—

We had gone to Portsmouth, leaving the King at
Weymouth, and were returning through the Needles,
when, as we got off Poole harbour, a small boat,
with three people in her, was seen a little on the
starboard bow. One man was rowing, the other
two persons were beckoning, evidently towards the
ship. As we drew near, we saw, through our
glasses, that the two people were an old man and
woman, and, as we appeared to be passing them,
their gestures became more and more vehement.
Many captains would have laughed, or taken no
notice of the old people. Not so Sir Harry—he
had a feeling for everyone. Ordering the ship to
be hove to, he allowed the boat to come alongside.

" Oh, captain, is our ain bairn Davie on board ?"
shouted the old people, in chorus.

Sir Harry, with the benignant smile his countenance so often wore, directed that they might be
assisted up the side.

" Who is it you want, good people ?" he asked, as
soon as their feet were safely planted on the deck,
where they stood, gazing round with astonished
countenances.

" Our ain son, Davie—David Campbell, sir," was
again the reply.

" Is there any man of that name on board ?"
inquired Sir Harry. " Let him be called aft."

A stout lad soon made his appearance, and was
immediately pressed in the old people's arms. This
son was a truant, long absent from his home. At
length, grown weary at delay, quitting their abode
near Edinburgh, they had travelled south, inquiring
at every port for their lost son, and only that morning had they arrived by waggon at Poole, believing
that it was a port where men-of-war were to be
found. A boatman, for the sake of a freight, had

persuaded them to come off with him, pointing out the ship which was then coming out through the Needles.

Sir Harry was so pleased with the perseverance and affection which the old couple had exhibited, that he took them on to Weymouth, when the story was told to the King. His Majesty had them presented to him, and he and Queen Charlotte paid them all sorts of attention, and at length, after they had spent some weeks with their son, dismissed them, highly gratified, to their home in the North.

Queen Charlotte was as good a woman as ever lived, and, in her way, was as kind and affable as was the King. She had a quaint humour about her, too, which frequently exhibited itself, in spite of the somewhat painful formality of the usual court circle. As an example—Sir Harry had had a present of bottled green peas made to him the previous year, and, looking on them as a great rarity, he had kept them to be placed on the table before his royal guests. As he knew more about ploughing the ocean than ploughing the land, and affairs nautical than horticultural, it did not occur to him that fresh green peas were to obtained on shore. The bottled green peas were therefore proudly produced on the first opportunity.

"Your Majesty," said Sir Harry, as the Queen was served, "those green peas have been kept a whole year."

The Queen made no reply till she had eaten a few, and sent several flying off from the prongs of her fork. Then, nodding with a smile, she quietly said, "So I did tink."

To the end of his days, Sir Harry used to laugh over the story, adding, "Sure enough, they were very green ; but as hard as swan-shot."

But I undertook to narrate a circumstance which exhibited Sir Harry Burrard Neale's character in its true colours. I need not enter into an account of that painful event, the Mutiny of the British Fleet. It broke out first at Spithead, on the 15th April, 1797, on board Lord Bridport's flag-ship, the *Royal George;* the crews of the other ships of the fleet following the example thus set them. The men, there can be no doubt, had very considerable grievances of which to complain; nor can it be well explained how, in those days, they could by legal means have had them redressed. One thing only is certain, mutiny was not the proper way of proceeding. We were at Spithead, and not an officer in the fleet knew what was about to occur, when, on the 14th, two of our men desired to speak with the captain, and then gave him the astounding intelligence that the ships' companies of the whole fleet had bound themselves to make certain important demands, and which, if not granted, that they would refuse to put to sea. The two men—they were quartermasters—moreover, stated that they had themselves been chosen delegates to represent the ship's company of the *San Fiorenzo*, by the rest of the fleet, but that they could assure him that all the men would prove true and loyal, and would obey their officers as far as was consistent with prudence.

Sir Harry thanked them, assuring them, in return, that he would trust them thoroughly. He, however, scarcely believed at that time the extent to which the mischief had gone. The next day evidence was given of the wide spread of the disaffection. Affairs day after day grew worse and worse; and although some of the superior officers acted with great judgment and moderation, others very nearly drove matters to the greatest extremity.

G

Meantime, the delegates of the *San Fiorenzo* attended the meetings of the mutineers, and, though at the imminent risk of their lives, regularly brought Sir Harry information of all that occurred. He transmitted it to the Admiralty, and it was chiefly through his representations and advice that conciliatory measures were adopted by the Government. Nearly all the just demands of the seamen having been granted, they returned to their duty, and it was supposed that the mutiny was at an end. Just before this, the Princess Royal had married the Duke of Wirtemberg, and the *San Fiorenzo* had been appointed to carry Her Royal Highness over to Cuxhaven. We could not, however, move without permission from the delegates. This was granted. Our upper-deck guns were stowed below, and the larger portion of the upper-deck fitted with cabins. In this condition, when arriving at Sheerness, we found to our surprise that the red flag was still flying on board the guardship, the *Sandwich.* Supposing that her crew had not been informed of what had taken place at Spithead, Sir Harry sent our delegates on board her, that they might explain the real state of affairs. The disgust of our men was very great when they were informed that fresh demands had been made by the crews of the North Sea fleet, of so frivolous a nature that it was not probable they would be granted. Our men, in spite of the character of delegates, which had been forced on them, could not help showing their indignation, and expressing themselves in no very courteous terms. This showed the mutineers that they were not over-zealous in their cause, and our people were warned that, should they prove treacherous, they and their ship would be sent to the bottom.

On returning on board, they informed Sir Harry of all that had occurred. Our delegates, at his suggestion, immediately communicated with those of the *Clyde*, an old fellow-cruiser, commanded by Captain Cunningham. That officer, on account of his justice, humanity, and bravery, enjoyed, as did Sir Harry, the confidence of his ship's company. An arrangement was therefore made between the captains and their crews that, should the mutineers persevere in their misconduct, they would take the ships out from amidst the fleet, fighting our way, if necessary, and run for protection under cover of the forts at Sheerness. Every preparation was made. We waited till the last moment. The mutineers showed no disposition to return to their duty. The *Clyde* was the in-shore ship; she was therefore to move first.* We watched her with intense interest, while we remained still as death. Not one of our officers appeared on deck, and but few of the men, though numerous eager eyes were gazing through the ports. The *Clyde* had springs on her cables, we knew, but as yet not a movement was perceptible. Suddenly her seamen swarmed on the yards, the topsails were let fall and sheeted home. She canted the right way. Hurrah! all sail was made. Away she went; and, before one of the mutinous fleet could go in chase, she was under the protection of the guns on shore. It was now our turn; but we had not a moment to lose, as the tide was on the turn to ebb, when we should have had it against us. What was our vexation, therefore, when the order was given to get under weigh, to find that the pilot,

---

* The plan was proposed and executed by the late Mr. W. Bardo, pilot, then a mate in the navy. He returned to the *San Fiorenzo*, and piloted her as he had the *Clyde*, when her own pilot refused to take charge.

either from fear, incompetency, or treachery, had declared that he could not take charge of the ship! Sir Harry would have taken her out himself; but the delay was fatal to his purpose, and before we could have moved, boats from the other ships were seen approaching the *San Fiorenzo*. They contained the delegates from the fleet, who, as they came up the side, began, with furious looks, to abuse our men for not having fired into the *Clyde*, and prevented her escaping. High words ensued, and so enraged did our men become at being abused because they did not fire on friends and countrymen, that one of the quartermasters, John Aynsley by name, came aft to the first lieutenant, and entreated that they might be allowed " to heave the blackguards overboard."

A nod from him would have sealed the fate of the delegates. I thought then (and I am not certain that I was wrong) that we might at that moment have seized the whole of the scoundrels, and carried them off prisoners to Sheerness. It would have been too great a risk to have run them up to the yardarm, or hove them overboard, as our men wished, lest their followers might have retaliated on the officers in their power.

No man was more careful of human life than Sir Harry, and it was a plan to which he would never have consented. The delegates, therefore, carried things with a high hand, and, convinced that our crew were loyal to their king and country, they ordered us to take up a berth between the *Inflexible* and *Director*, to unbend our sails, and to send our powder on board the *Sandwich*, at the masthead of which ship the flag of the so-called Admiral Parker was then flying. That man, Richard Parker, had been shipmate with a considerable number of the crew of the *San Fiorenzo*, as acting lieutenant, but had been dismissed his ship for drunkenness, and having lost all hope of promotion, had entered before the mast.

Our people had, therefore, a great contempt for him, and said that he was no sailor, and that his conduct had ever been unlike that of an officer and a gentleman. Such a man, knowing that he acted with a rope round his neck, was of course the advocate of the most desperate measures. Everything that took place was communicated immediately to Sir Harry, who advised the men to pretend compliance, and, much to our relief, the other delegates took their departure. As soon as they were gone, Sir Harry told the ship's company that, provided they would agree to stand by him, he would take the ship into Sheerness, as before intended. The men expressed their readiness to incur every possible risk to effect that purpose. The almost unarmed condition of the ship at the time must be remembered. The men set zealously to work to prepare for the enterprise. Springs were got on our cables. All was ready. The flood had made. The object was to cast in-shore. The men were at their stations. We were heaving on the spring—it broke at the most critical moment, and we cast outward. There was no help for it. Nothing could prevent us from running right in among the two ships of the mutinous fleet which I have mentioned, and which lay with their guns double shotted, and the men at quarters, with the lanyards in their hands, ready to fire at us. Our destruction seemed certain; but not for a moment did our captain lose his presence of mind. Calm as ever, he ordered the quartermaster Aynsley to appear on deck as if in command, while the officers concealed themselves in different parts of

the ship, he standing where he could issue his orders
and watch what was taking place. All was sheeted
home in a moment, and we stood in between the
two line-of-battle ships, the *Director* and *Inflexible*.
The ship, by this time, had got good way on her.
It appeared that we were about to take up the berth
into which we had been ordered, when Sir Harry
directed that all the sheets should suddenly be let
fly. This took the mutineers so completely by surprise, that not a gun was then fired at us. Sir
Harry next ordered the helm to be put "hard-a
port," which caused the ship to shoot a-head of the
Inflexible—we were once more outside our enemies.
Springing immediately on deck, he took the command, crying out, in his encouraging tone, "Well
done, my lads—well done!"

A loud murmur of applause and satisfaction was
heard fore and aft; but we had no time for a cheer.

"Now clear away the bulkheads, and mount the
guns," he added.

Every man flew with a hearty will to obey his
orders. And need there was; for scarcely were the
words out of his mouth than the whole fleet of
thirty-two sail opened their fire on us. The shot
flew like hail around us, and thick as hail, ploughing
up the water as they leaped along it, chasing each
other across the surface on every side of the ship.
We could have expected nothing else than to be sunk
instantly, had we had time for consideration; but,
as it was, wonderfully few struck our hull, while not
a shroud was cut away, nor was a man hurt. The
huge *Director*, close to us, might have sent us to
the bottom with a broadside, but not a shot from
her, that we could see, came aboard us.

"They have not the heart to fire at us, the blackguards!" observed one of the men near me.

"It may be that, Bill; but, to my mind, they're struck all of a heap at seeing the brave way our captain did that," answered another. "If we'd had the guns mounted he'd have fired smack into them. We send our powder aboard that pirate Parker's ship! we unbend our sails to please such a sneaking scoundrel as he!"

"It's just this, that the misguided chaps are slaves against their will, and they haven't become bad enough yet to fire on their countrymen, and maybe old friends and shipmates," said a third.

Such were the opinions generally expressed on board. It was reported afterwards that the *Director* fired blank cartridges, and this may have been the case, but I think more probably that her people were first struck with astonishment at our manœuvre, and then, with admiration at the bravery displayed, purposely fired wide of us. As, however, we were frequently struck, some shots by traitorous hands must have been aimed at us from her, or from some of the other ships. In little more than two hours the bulkheads were cleared away from the cabin door, to the break of the quarter-deck (the whole space having, as I before said, been fitted up with cabins for the suite of Her Royal Highness). The guns on both sides were got up from the hold and mounted, and we were ready for action. As soon as the task was accomplished, the men came aft in a body, and entreated, should any ships be sent after us by the mutineers, that they might be allowed to fight to the last, and go down with our colours flying, rather than yield, and return to the fleet at the Nore.

Sir Harry readily promised not to disappoint their wishes.

We stood on, but as yet no sign was perceptible

of chase being made after us. It was possible, we thought, that no ship's company could be induced to weigh in pursuit. They well knew that we should prove a tough bargain, had any single ship come up with us. Should we prove victorious, every man might have been hung as a pirate. As to Parker, he dared not leave his fleet, as he ventured to call it.

Our master, although a good navigator, did not feel himself justified in taking charge of the ship, within the boundaries of a Branch pilot, and we were therefore on the look-out for a pilot vessel, when a lugger was discovered on the lee-bow, and we were on the point of bearing down to her, when we made out first a ship or two, then several sail, and lastly, a whole fleet, which we guessed must be the North Sea Fleet standing for the Nore. We were steering for them, to give the admiral notice of what had occurred, when the red flag was discovered flying on board them also. They had, as it appeared, left their station in a state of mutiny, having placed the admiral and all the officers under arrest. To avoid them altogether was impossible, and before long a frigate bore down to us. Should our real character be discovered, we must be captured by an over-whelming force. Still Sir Harry remained calm and self-possessed as ever. As the frigate approached, he ordered all the officers below, and giving the speaking-trumpet to Stanley, the quartermaster, told him to reply as he might direct. The frigate hailed and inquired what we were about. "Looking out to stop ships with provisions, that we may supply the fleet," was the answer. The people of the frigate, satisfied with this reply, proceeded to rejoin the fleet, while we, glad to escape further questioning, made sail in chase of the lugger. She was a fast craft, and led us a chase of four hours before we captured her. She proved to be the *Castor and Pollux* privateer of sixteen guns. Having taken out the prisoners, and put a prize crew on board, we were proceeding to Portsmouth, when the lugger, being to windward, spoke a brig, which had left that place the day before, and from her gained the information that the mutiny had again broken out at Spithead. Under these circumstances, Sir Harry thought it prudent to anchor under Dungeness until he could communicate with the Admiralty.

This we did; but it was a time of great anxiety, for the mutineers might consider it important to capture us, to hold Sir Harry and his officers as hostages, and to wreak their vengeance on our men. We got springs on the cable, and the ship ready for action. During the middle watch a ship was made out bearing down towards us; she was high out of the water, and was pronounced by many to be a line-of-battle ship. Sir Harry was on deck in an instant—the private signal was made—would it be answered? Yes; but there was no security in this, as, should the ship's company have mutinied, they would naturally have possessed themselves of it. The drum beat to quarters, the fighting lanterns were up, their light streaming through our ports. Our men earnestly repeated their request to be allowed to sink rather than surrender to the mutineers. No sight of the sort could be finer, as the brave fellows stood stripped to the waist, dauntless and resolute, not about to fight with a common foe, but one that would prove cruel and revengeful in the extreme. The wind was extremely light, and the stranger closed very slowly. The suspense was awful. In a short time we might be engaged in a deadly struggle with a vastly superior foe, and deadly

all determined that it should be. Nearer and nearer
the stranger drew; at length our captain hailed.
The answer came: "The *Huzzar!* Lord Garlais!
from the West Indies." She anchored close to us,
and we exchanged visits. Her people, ignorant of
the mutiny, could not understand the necessity of
the precaution we had taken. They were so struck,
when made acquainted with what had occurred, at
the bravery and determination of our ship's company, that they immediately swore they would stick
by us, and that, should any ship be sent to take us
back to the Nore, they would share our fate, whatever that might be. I am sure that they would
have proved as good as their word, but daylight
came, and no enemy appeared. We lay here for
some time, that Sir Harry might ascertain what was
occurring on shore. He found that most active and
energetic measures were being taken to repress the
mutiny, and in a few days we heard that the ship's
company of the *Sandwich* had taken her into Sheerness, and allowed their late leader, Parker, to be
arrested by a guard of soldiers, sent on board for
that purpose by Admiral Buckner. We sailed for
Plymouth, and another ship was appointed to have
the honour of taking over the Princess Royal.

I must say a word or two about that mutiny. I
am convinced that the proportion of disaffected men
was comparatively small. The seamen had grievances, but those would have been redressed without
their proceeding to the extremities into which they
plunged, led by a few disappointed and desperate
men like Parker. Had greater energy been shown
from the first, during some of the opportunities
which occurred, the whole affair might have been
concluded in a more dignified manner, at a much
earlier date. I will instance one occasion. Having

one day got leave from the delegates of our ship, while we lay off Sheerness, to go on shore, I landed at the dockyard. I found, as I passed through it, that I was followed by the whole body of delegates, walking two-and-two in procession, Parker and Davis leading, arm-in-arm. Just as we got outside the gates, the Lancashire Fencibles appeared, coming to strengthen the garrison. As soon as the seamen got near the soldiers, they began to abuse them in so scurrilous a manner, that the officer in command halted his men, and seeing the admiral and super-intendent, close to whom I at the time was standing opposite the gates, he came, and, complaining of the insults offered to himself and men, asked permission to surround and capture them. So eager did I feel, that I involuntarily exclaimed, "Yes! yes! now's the time!" The admiral, on hearing me, turned sharply round, and demanded how I dared to speak in that way? "Because there they all are, sir, and we may have them in a bunch!" I replied, pointing to Parker, Davis, and the rest. The admiral told me that I did not know what I was saying; but I did, and I have no cause to suppose that I was wrong.

When the truly loyal and heroic conduct of our ship's company became known, it was intended to raise a sum in every seaport town in England to present to them. From some reason, however, the Government put a stop to it, and the only subscription received was from Ludlow in Shropshire, from whence the authorities sent £500 to Sir Harry Neale, which he distributed to the ship's company on the quarter-deck.

Orlo and Era:

A TALE OF THE AFRICAN SLAVE TRADE.

THERE exists an extensive district on the west coast of Africa, about forty miles to the north of the far-famed river Niger, known as the Yoruba country. Sixty years ago it was one of the most thickly populated and flourishing parts of equatorial Africa, the inhabitants having also attained to a considerable amount of civilization, and made fair progress in many industrial arts.

Then came those dreadful wars, carried on by the more powerful and cruel chiefs, for the purpose of making slaves to sell to the white traders, who carried them away to toil in the plantations of North and South America and Cuba, and the prosperity of the once happy people of Yoruba was brought to an end. The savage rulers of Dahomey and Lagos now became notorious for the barbarities they inflicted on the unoffending tribes in their neighbourhood. The Yoruba country was the chief scene of their hunting expeditions. Towns and villages were attacked and burned; the able-bodied men and young women and children were carried off into slavery; the aged were ruthlessly murdered, fields and plantations were laid waste, and a howling wilderness was left behind. At length the scattered remnants of the population who had escaped from slavery and death assembled together in a spot among rocks, especially strong by nature, where they hoped to be able to make a stand against their persecutors. Here they built a town, to which they gave the name of Abbeokuta, or the place among the rocks. It increased rapidly in population and extent, for numerous were the unfortunates in search of a home, and rest, and peace.

Lagos, one of the chief strongholds of the slave-dealers, which the Yorubans most had to fear, has since been taken possession of by the British, and has been declared an English colony or settlement; but Dahomey, governed by its bloodthirsty monarch, with his army of six thousand Amazons and five thousand male warriors, still exists as a terrible scourge to the surrounding territories.

On the confines of the Yoruba country existed a beautiful village which had hitherto escaped the ravages of the relentless slave-hunting foe. It was situated on the banks of a rapid stream, which gave freshness to the air, and fertility to the neighbouring plantations. Palms, dates, and other trees of tropical growth, overshadowed the leaf-thatched cottages, in which truly peace and plenty might be said to reign. Although true happiness cannot exist where Christianity is not, and where the fear of the fetish and the malign influence of the spirit of evil rules supreme over the mind, the people were contented, and probably as happy as are any of the countless numbers of the still benighted children of Africa. Rumours of wars and slave-hunts reached them, but they had so long escaped the inflictions others had suffered, that they flattered themselves they should escape altogether. So little accustomed are the negro race to look to the future, contented with the pleasures of the passing moment, that as they did not actually see the danger, they allowed no anticipation of evil to mar their happiness. The hearts of the dark-skinned children of that burning clime are as susceptible of the tender sentiments of love and friendship as many of those boasting a higher degree of civilization, and a complexion of a fairer hue. No couple, indeed, could have been more warmly attached than were young Orlo and Era, who had lately become man and wife, and taken up their abode in the village. They were industrious and happy, and from morning till night their voices might be heard singing as they went about their daily work. Orlo employed himself principally in collecting the various products of the country to sell to the traders who occasionally visited the district,—palm oil, and gold dust from the neighbouring rivulet, and elephants' tusks, and skins which he took in the chase.

At length Era gave birth to a child, a little boy, which proved a great addition to their happiness; and drew still closer the bonds of their affection. Indeed no people can be fonder of their children than are the negroes of Africa.

Soon after little Sobo was born Orlo set off on a hunting expedition with several other villagers, telling Era that he must get her some fresh soft skins for their child's bed, and that he must be more industrious than ever, as he had a family to provide for.

Era entreated him not to be long away.

"Two or three days will see me back, laden with the spoils of the chase," was his answer, in a cheerful tone.

Era's heart sank within her—why, she could not

tell. With anxious eyes she watched him and his companions as, with bows, and arrows, and lances in hand, they disappeared among the trees.

Seldom had Orlo and his party been more successful. More than one lion, several antelopes, and numerous monkeys were killed. Even a huge elephant was conquered by their skill and cunning. The skins of the animals slaughtered were hidden in safe places, to be taken up on their return. Excited by their success they proceeded even farther than they intended. Night surprised them, and collecting together they formed a camp, with fires blazing in the centre to keep off the savage beasts roaming around.

Their supper having been discussed, they were merrily laughing and talking over their adventures when they were startled by some terrific shouts and cries close to them. They grasped their arms, but before a bow could be drawn a body of warriors rushed in on them with clubs and swords, knocking over or cutting down all who stood at bay or attempted resistance. Some endeavoured to escape, but they were completely surrounded. Several were killed by their savage assailants, and their bodies were left where they fell. The greater number were secured with their arms bound tightly behind them, and they found themselves captives to the troops of the King of Dahomey, towards whose capital they were marched away in triumph. They had heard enough of the fate which had befallen so many of their countrymen to know that they must never more expect to taste the sweets of liberty ; but they were scarcely aware of the horrible cruelty to which the will of the tyrant King of Dahomey might compel some of them to submit. Bitter, too, was the anguish which poor Orlo suffered when he felt that he should for ever be separated from his beloved Era.

The journey was long and tedious, and the captives' feet were torn by the thorns and cut by the hard rocks over which they had to pass ; but whenever they lagged behind they were urged on by the long spears of their relentless captors. Arrived at the capital, they were astonished at its extent and the number of its inhabitants, and, more than all, by the vast army they saw drawn up for the inspection of the king. They had little opportunity of seeing much, for they were soon conducted into a large low building, where they were secured by iron shackles, back to back, to a long beam, scarcely able to move.

After remaining here for several days Orlo and others were separated from their companions and carried to a building on one side of the great square of the city, where all public ceremonies were performed. Dreadful shrieks assailed their ears both by day and night. They heard they were uttered by the human victims offered up by the savage king to the spirits of his departed ancestors.

They were not long left in doubt as to what was to be their fate. They also were to be destroyed in the same manner. Some of their number on hearing this sank into a state of apathy, others loudly bemoaned their cruel lot, and others plotted how they might escape, but Orlo could think only of his beloved Era, and the anxiety and anguish his absence would have caused her.

At length Orlo and nine others were taken out and told they were to enjoy the high privilege of being sacrificed in presence of their king. They were now dressed in white garments, and tall red caps were put on their heads. Their arms and legs were then bound securely, and they were placed in a sitting posture in small canoe-shaped troughs, and thus in a long procession were carried around the square amid the cruel shouts of the savage populace. At length they reached a high platform or slope in the centre of the square, on which sat the king, under the shade of a vast umbrella, surrounded by his courtiers and chiefs. Below the platform were collected a vast mob of savages, their hideous countenances looking up with fierce delight at the terrible drama which was to be enacted. Among the crowd stood several men of gigantic stature, even more savage-looking than the rest, armed with huge knotted clubs. These they knew instinctively were their intended executioners. Not one of them attempted to plead for mercy; that they knew were vain. Their eyes glanced hopelessly round, now on the assembled throng below, now on the groups collected on the platform, not expecting to meet a look of compassion turned towards them. But yes, among one group they see a man of strange appearance. His skin is white, and by his fine dress, glittering with gold, they believe him to be a great chief. He advances towards the king, whom, with eager look, he addresses in a strange language. What he says they cannot tell, till another man of their own colour speaks, and then they know that he is pleading for their lives; not only pleading, but offering a large ransom if they be given up to him. How anxiously they listen for the reply! The king will not hear of it. The spirit of his father complains that he has been neglected; that his nation must have become degenerate; that they have ceased to conquer, since so few captives have been sent to bear him company in the world of shades. Again the strange white chief speaks, and offers higher bribes. Curious that he should take so much trouble about some poor black captives they think. What can be his object? What can influence him?

He does not plead altogether in vain. The king will give him four for the sum he offers, but no more. He would not dare thus to displease the shade of his father, and the white chief may choose whom he will. The victims gaze anxiously at his countenance. It is merciful and benign they think —unlike any they have before seen. Which of them will he select?

He does not hesitate; he knows what must be passing in the hearts of those poor wretches. He quickly lays his hand on four of them, and turns away his head with sorrow from the rest. Orlo is among those he has claimed. They show but little pleasure or gratitude as they are released, and, being stripped of their sacrificial garments, are placed under charge of his attendants. The rest of the miserable captives are held up, some by men, others by the Amazonian warriors, to the gaze of the expectant multitude, who shriek and shout horribly, and then they are cast forward into the midst of the crowd, when the executioners set on them with their clubs and speedily terminate their sufferings. For several successive days is the same horrible scene enacted, the Fetish men declaring that the spirit of the late king is not yet satisfied.

Orlo by degrees recovered from the stupor into which his sufferings, mental and bodily, and the anticipation of a cruel death had thrown him. He then found that the white chief, whose slave he considered himself, was no other than the captain of a British man-of-war, cruising off the coast for the suppression of the slave trade—not that he understood very clearly much about the matter, but he

had heard of the sea, and that big canoes floated on
it which carried his countrymen across it to a land
from which none ever came back. Still, as this
captain had certainly saved his life, he felt an affection for him, and hoped that he should be allowed
to remain his slave, and not be sold to a stranger.
As to asking to be liberated to be sent back to Era,
he did not for a moment suppose that such a
request would be granted, and he therefore did not
make it. At last the coast was reached, and a ship
appeared, and a boat came and took them on board.
The captain had seen something in Orlo's countenance which especially pleased him, so he asked
whether he would like to remain with him ; and
Orlo, very much surprised that the option should be
given him, said, " Yes, certainly."

So Orlo was entered on the ship's books, and soon
learned not only to attend on the captain, but to be
a sailor. His affection for his patron and preserver
was remarkable. Whatever Captain Fisher wished
he attempted to perform to the best of his ability,
while he was attentive and faithful in the extreme.
He soon acquired enough English to make himself
understood, while he could comprehend everything
that was said to him.

The *Sea Sprite* was a very fast sailing corvette,
and had already, by her speed and the sagacity with
which her cruising-ground was selected, made more
captures than any other craft of the squadron. Her
success continued after Orlo had become one of her
crew. He always got leave to go on board the
prizes when they were taken possession of, and his
services were soon found of value as interpreter.
His object was naturally to inquire about news from
his own part of the country. He was not likely to
obtain any satisfactory information. Some time

passed—another capture was made. He returned on board the corvette very depressed in spirits, and was often seen in tears. Captain Fisher asked him the cause of his sorrows. He had learned that at length his own village had been surprised during the night by the slave-hunters of the King of Dahomey, that not one of the inhabitants had escaped, and that all had been carried off into captivity. They had been sold to different dealers, and had been transported to the baracoons on different parts of the coast, ready for embarkation. Where Era had been carried he could not ascertain; only one thing was certain—she and her child had been seen in the hands of the Dahomian soldiers, on their way to the capital. His beloved Era was then a slave; and he by this time full well knew what slavery meant. He had seen several slave ships captured, and the horrors, the barbarities, and indignities to which the captives on board were exposed. He pictured to himself the terrible journey from the interior, the lash of the brutal driver descending on her shoulders as she tottered on with her infant in her arms, her knees bending from weakness, her feet torn with thorns and hard rocks—she who had been so tenderly cared for—whom he loved so dearly;—the thought was more than he could bear. He looked over the side of the ship, and gazed at the blue waters, and said to himself, "I shall find rest beneath them; in the world of spirits I shall meet my own Era, and be happy."

One of the officers of the ship, a Christian man, had watched him. He had before observed his melancholy manner, so different to what he had at first exhibited. Lieutenant L—— called him, and asked him the cause of his sorrow.

Orlo narrated his simple history.

"And no one has thought all this time of imparting any knowledge of Gospel truth to this poor African," said the lieutenant to himself; and a blush rose on his own cheeks. "No time shall be lost, though," he added; and he unfolded in language suited to his comprehension, and in all its simplicity, the grand scheme of redemption whereby sinning man can be accepted by a holy and just God as freed from sin, through the great sacrifice offered once on the Cross.

Orlo listened eagerly and attentively. All ideas of suicide had left his mind. He longed to know more of this wonderful, this glorious news.

"Then, Orlo, would you not wish to please so merciful and kind a Master, who has done so much for you?" asked the lieutenant.

"Yes, massa, dat I would," answered the African.

"One way in which you can do so, is to bear patiently and humbly, as He did, the afflictions the loving God thinks fit to send. He does it in mercy, depend on that. God's ways are not our ways; but the all-powerful God who made the world must of necessity know better what is right and good than we poor frail dying creatures, whom He formed from the dust of the earth, and who, but for His will, would instantly return to dust again."

"Me see, me see," answered the negro, in a tone as joyful as if he had found a pearl of great price; and so he had, for he had found Gospel truth.

"God knows better than we," was his constant remark after this when he heard others complaining of the misfortunes and ills of life.

The ship had now been nearly her full time in commission, and her captain was in daily expectation of receiving orders to return home. Poor Orlo's heart sank within him. He must either quit his kind master and his still kinder lieutenant, or, by leaving the coast, abandon all hopes of ever again seeing his beloved Era. To be sure, he knew that she might long ere this have been carried off to the Brazils or Cuba; and faint indeed was the expectation that they ever should meet in this world. Then, again, another feeling arose: " I am now a Christian and she is still a heathen. How can God receive her in heaven?" But after a time he thought—" Ah, but I can pray that she may become a Christian. God's ways are not our ways. He will hear my prayers—that I know. He can bring about by some of His ways what I cannot accomplish." And Orlo prayed as he had never prayed before. Captain Fisher treated Orlo with unusual kindness, and, under the circumstances, he could not have been happier on board any ship in the navy.

Captain Fisher was not a man to relax in his efforts, as long as he remained on the station, to suppress the abominable traffic in human beings by all the means in his power. The *Sea Sprite* continued cruising, accordingly, along the coast, looking in at the different stations, till one morning, at daybreak, a suspicious schooner was seen at anchor, close in with the shore. The increasing light revealed the corvette to those on board. The schooner instantly slipped her cable and stood along the coast, while the *Sea Sprite* made all sail in chase. Of the character of the vessel there could be no doubt, or she would not have attempted to run from the man-of-war. The *Sea Sprite* stood as close in as the depth of water would allow; farther in she dare not go. There was still a possibility of the chase escaping. Orlo, as usual, was the most eager on board. He delighted in seeing his countrymen freed from slavery, and he never abandoned the hope of meeting with Era. "I pray I meet her. I know God hear prayer," said Orlo.

The wind fell. "Out boats," was the order. Captain Fisher went himself. The chase was a large schooner. A boat was seen to put off from her and pull towards the surf : whether or not she could get through it seemed a question. The English seamen bent to their oars ; they were resolved to reach the chase before she could again get the breeze. They dashed alongside, and soon sprang over her bulwarks. No resistance was made. Poor Orlo, glancing round, discovered, to his disappointment, that she had no slaves on board. The master, it was found, had landed with the specie for the purchase of slaves. One of the slave crew—a mate, he looked like—appeared to have a peculiar thickness under his knees ; Orlo detected it, and pointed it out to the captain. The master-at-arms was ordered to examine him. Most unwillingly the fellow tucked up his trousers—grinning horribly at Orlo all the time—when he was found to have on a pair of garters, out of each of which rolled thirty doubloons.

The schooner's head being put off-shore, the boats took her in tow, till, a breeze springing up, sail was made on her for Sierra Leone. The next morning commenced with a thick mist and rain. Orlo, from his quickness of vision, was now constantly employed as one of the look-outs. He was on the watch to go aloft directly it gave signs of clearing. His impatience, however, did not allow him to remain till the mist dispersed. Away aloft he went, observing, "It must fine soon ; den I see sip." He had not been many minutes at the masthead when he shouted, "Sip in-shore?" He had discovered her royals above the mist. Sail was instantly made in chase. Some time elapsed before the *Sea Sprite* was discovered. Suddenly the mist cleared, and there appeared close in-shore a large American slave ship. There was no doubt about her, with her great beam and wide spread of canvas.

Hoisting American colours, the stranger made all sail to escape. He was standing off the land ; but as on that course he would have had to pass unpleasantly near the corvette, he tacked in-shore, and then bore away along the surf, hoping thus, with his large sails, to draw ahead and escape. The light wind appeared to favour him, but Captain Fisher determined that it should not. Ordering the boats away, he took one with a strongly-armed crew, and pulled to windward to cut off the chase, while two others went to leeward, so that his chance of escaping was small indeed. The slave captain seemed to think so likewise. He dared not meet in fight the true-hearted British seaman. Regardless of the risk he and his own crew would run, of the destruction he was about to bring on hundreds of his fellow-creatures, the savage slave captain put up his helm, and ran the ship under all sail towards the shore.

"What is the fellow about?" exclaimed Captain Fisher. "If that ship is full, as she seems to be, she has not less than four or five hundred human beings on board, and he'll run the risk of drowning every one of them."

It was too evident, however, that this was the design of the slaver's captain. His heart was seared. Long accustomed to human suffering in every possible form, he set no more value on the lives of his cargo than if they had been so many sheep, except so far as they could be exchanged for all-potent dollars. On flew the beautiful fabric—for beautiful she was, in spite of her nefarious employment—to destruction. With all her sails set, through the roaring surf she dashed, then rose on the summit of a sea, and down she came, striking heavily, her ropes flying wildly and her sails flapping furiously in the breeze. What mattered it to the slaver's crew that they left their hapless passengers to perish! Their boats were lowered, and, with such valuables as they could secure, and some of the slaves which, for their greater value, they wished to save, they made their escape to shore, leaving the ship, with the American colours flying, to her fate.

Captain Fisher and the other boats now closed with the wreck, while the corvette also was standing in. When close as she could venture to come, she anchored, and the master came off from her in a whale-boat and joined the other boats. Terrible was the sight which now met the eyes of the English seamen. Orlo beheld it, too, with horror and anguish. As the ship rolled fearfully from side to side, the terrified negroes forced their way up on deck, and in their wild despair, not knowing what to do, many leaped into the raging breakers which swept by alongside, and, helplessly whirling round and round, were soon hidden beneath the waves. One after the other the poor wretches rushed up on deck; many, following the impulse of the first, leaped overboard to meet a like speedy death; others, clinging to the wreck, were washed overboard; some of the stronger still clung on; but many yet remained below.

"This is sad work," exclaimed Captain Fisher. "We must save these poor people at all hazards."

A cheer was the reply, and, the men giving way, the boats dashed at great hazard through the surf to leeward of the wreck ; but here it seemed almost impossible to board her from the heavy lurches she was making, sending the blocks and spars and rigging flying over their heads, and threatening to swamp the boats should they get alongside.   Still Captain Fisher and his gallant followers persevered. He was the first on board, and Orlo leaped on the deck after him.   The scene appeared even more horrible than at a distance.   The negroes, as they could get clear of their manacles, climbed up from the slave deck, and ran to and fro, shrieking and crying out like people deprived of reason.   Some ran on till they sprang overboard ; others turned again, and continued running backwards and forwards, till the seamen were compelled to catch them and throw them below till the boats could be got ready for their rescue.   The captain ordered Orlo to try and pacify them.   He answered, that their extreme terror arose from the idea which the slaver's crew had given them, that the object of the English in taking possession of the vessel was to cut all their throats.   Orlo did his best to quiet their fears when he learned the cause, assuring them the reason the British seaman had come on board was to do them good, and to try and save their lives.   It was some time, however, before they would credit his assertions. The ship's barge had now been brought in and anchored just outside the rollers, while the cutter was backed in under the slaver's counter.   Three of the slaves at a time were then allowed to come up, and were lowered into the boat, from which the whale-boat took them through the surf to the barge, and that when full ultimately carried them to the corvette.   The process was of necessity slow, the toil was excessive, and the danger very great ; but the British seamen did not shrink from it.   Orlo had from the first, while acting as interpreter, been scanning the countenances of all he met, making inquiries of those who could understand his language (for all could not do so) if they could give him any information about his beloved Era. Again and again he went below, but the darkness prevented him from distinguishing any one, and the shrieks, groans, and cries from making his voice heard, or from hearing what any one might have said.

Night closed on the hitherto unremitting labours of the gallant crew. They had thus saved two hundred poor wretches, but upwards of two hundred remained on board when darkness made it impossible to remove them. Still, could they be left to perish, which they probably would if left alone? The slaver's crew might return, and either attempt to land them, to keep them in captivity, or burn the ship, to prevent them from falling into the hands of the British. The risk of remaining was very great, but several officers volunteered. Orlo's friend, Lieutenant ——, claimed the privilege, and Orlo begged that he might remain with him. The last performance of the boats was to bring off some rice which had been found in the captured schooner, and cooked, thoughtfully, by the captain's orders, in his coppers, in readiness for the liberated negroes. Plenty of men were ready to remain with Lieutenant ——. Without this supply of food, few, probably, of the slaves on board would have survived the night; even as it was, many of those who were rescued died on their passage to the corvette, or on her decks. Lieutenant —— and his brave companions had truly a night of trial. The wind increased, the surf roared louder and louder as it broke around them, the ship rolled and struck more and more violently, till it seemed impossible that she could hold together, while all this time the unhappy captives below were shrieking and crying out most piteously for help. Poor creatures! they knew not how to pray, or to whom to pray. They thought and believed, and not without reason, that a Fetish, or spirit of evil, had got possession of them, and was wreaking his malice on their heads. Orlo gladly, by the lieutenant's orders, went frequently below to try and comfort them, and to assure them that by the return of daylight fresh efforts would be made for their rescue. Still great indeed were their sufferings. Many, both men, women, and children, died during that fearful night, from wet, cold, fear, and hunger, as they sat, still closely packed on the slave deck. Orlo's kind heart made him suffer almost as much as they were doing—the more so that he felt how little could be done to relieve them.

At length the morning dawned, when it was found that the ship had driven considerably farther in towards the beach. As daylight broke, people were seen collecting on the shore; their numbers increased; they were gesticulating violently. Did they come to render assistance to their perishing fellow-countrymen? No; led on by the miscreant whites who had formed the crew of the slave ship, and deceived by their falsehoods, they had come to attempt the recapture of the ship. The corvette had, of necessity, stood off-shore for the night. Lieutenant ——, hoisting a signal of distress, prepared to defend the prize to the last. He examined the shore anxiously. The slaver's crew and their black allies were bringing boats or canoes to launch, for the purpose of attacking the ship. Should the wretches succeed, he knew that his life and that of all his companions would be sacrificed.

At length the corvette was seen working up under all sail. She approached ; her anchor was dropped, and her boats, being lowered, pulled in towards the wreck. As they got near, the people on shore, balked in their first project, opened a hot fire of musketry on them. The boats had not come unarmed. The larger ones were immediately anchored, and, each having a gun of some weight, opened a hot fire on the beach. This was more than the slave dealers had bargained for. They were ready enough to kill others, but had no fancy to be killed themselves. Several times the blacks took to flight, but were urged back again by the white men, till, some of the shot taking effect on them, the beach was at last cleared.

The wreck was now again boarded. Lieutenant —— and his men were found almost worn out; the hold was full of water, and the ship was giving signs of breaking up. No time was to be lost. The larger boats anchored, as before, outside the rollers, and, by means of the smaller ones, communication by ropes being established, the negroes were, a few at a time, hauled through the surf. Many were more dead than alive, and several died before they reached the corvette. Some were brought up by their companions dead, and many were the heart-rending scenes where fathers and mothers found that they had lost their children, husbands their wives, or children their parents. Orlo had held out bravely all the night, but his strength, towards the morning, gave way, and Lieutenant ——, seeing his condition, directed that he should be carried back to the corvette, which he reached in an almost unconscious state.

This living cargo was composed of all ages. There were strong men and youths, little boys, women, young girls, and children, and several mothers with infants at their breasts. How fondly and tenderly the poor creatures pressed them there, and endeavoured to shelter them from the salt spray and cold! Fully two hundred were carried on board the corvette during the morning, and it was found that the immortal spirits of nearly fifty of those who had been left on board during the night had passed away. The last poor wretch being rescued, the wreck was set on fire, both fore and aft; the flames burst quickly forth, surrounding the masts, from which still floated that flag which, professing to be the flag of freedom, has so often protected that traffic which has carried thousands upon thousands of the human race into hopeless and abject slavery. The seamen instinctively gave a cheer as they saw it disappear among the devouring flames.

The labours of Captain Fisher and his brave crew were not over. They had to provide food and shelter for fully four hundred of the rescued negroes. Rice, as before, was boiled, and cocoa was given them, and those who most required care were clothed and carried to the galley fire to warm. Among the last rescued was a young woman with a little boy, on whom all her care was lavished. Though herself almost perished, before she would touch food she fed him, and when some clothing was given her she wrapped it round him. She had been found in the fore part of the ship in an almost fainting condition, where she had remained unnoticed, apparently in a state of stupor, with her little boy pressed to her heart. Orlo had been placed under the doctor's care. It was not till the next morning that he was allowed to come on deck, where his services were at once called into requisition as interpreter. Though unacquainted with the language of many of the tribes to which the captives belonged, he was generally able to make himself understood. A sail had been spread over part of the deck, beneath which the women and young children were collected. The doctor, when about to visit it, called Orlo to accompany him, as interpreter. Among them, sitting on the deck, and leaning against a gun carriage, with her arm thrown round the neck of a little boy, was a young woman, though wan and ill, still possessing that peculiar beauty occasionally seen among several of the tribes of Africa. Orlo fixed his eyes on her; his knees trembled; he rushed forward; she sprang up, uttering a wild shriek of joy, and his arms were thrown around her. He had found his long lost Era and their child. "Ah! God hear prayer; I know now!" he exclaimed joyfully. "Wife soon be Christian, and child. God berry, berry good!"

Happily, the next morning the corvette fell in with another man-of-war, between which and the schooner the rescued slaves being distributed, all three made sail for Sierra Leone. The blacks were there landed, and ground given them on which to settle. Orlo begged that he and Era and their child might also be there set on shore. He did not go empty-handed, for, besides pay and prize-money, generously advanced him by his captain, gifts were showered on him both by his officers and messmates, and he became one of the most flourishing settlers in that happy colony. At length, however, wishing once more to see his own people, and to assist in spreading the truth of the Gospel, which he had so sincerely embraced, among them, he removed to Abbeokuta, where, with his wife now a Christian woman, and surrounded by a young Christian family, he is now settled, daily setting forth, by his consistent walk, the beauties and graces of the Christian faith. Whenever any of his friends are in difficulties, he always says, "Ah! God hear prayer! You pray; never fear!"